Under
Pressure

Alan Gibbons is a full-time writer and a visiting speaker and lecturer
at schools, colleges and literary events nationwide, including the major
book festivals: Edinburgh, Northern Children's Book Festival, Swansea,
Cheltenham, Sheffield and Salford. Alan has recently embarked on a high
profile, nationwide campaign to champion libraries and librarianship and
to reevaluate government commitment to educational spending.

Also by Alan Gibbons:

Under Pressure

Alan Gibbons

Orion
Children's Books

First published in Great Britain in 1997
by Orion Children's Books
Reissued in Great Britain in 2010
by Orion Children's Books
a division of the Orion Publishing Group Ltd
Orion House
5 Upper St Martin's Lane
London WC2H 9EA
An Hachette UK company

The Orion Publishing Group's policy is to use papers that are natural, renewable and recyclable products and made from wood grown in sustainable forests. The logging and manufacturing processes are expected to conform to the environmental regulations of the country of origin.

978-1-4440-0176-1

A catalogue record for this book is available from the British Library.

www.orionbooks.co.uk

Rough Diamonds

THE SQUAD

Darren 'Daz' Kemble (goalkeeper)
Joey Bannen (defence and substitute goalkeeper)
Mattie Hughes (defence)
Anthony 'Ant' Glover (defence)
Jimmy Mintoe (defence)
Carl Bain (defence)
Gordon Jones (defence)
John O'Hara (midfield)
Jamie Moore (midfield or striker)
Kevin 'Guv' McGovern (midfield or striker, and captain)
Bashir Gulaid (midfield)
Pete 'Ratso' Ratcliffe (midfield)
Dave Lafferty (striker)

Manager: Ronnie Mintoe

PART ONE

Pressure

One

The pain barrier – that's where I begin. Oh, think I'm all talk, do you? Then you don't know me very well. Let me introduce myself, I'm Kev McGovern – the Guv'nor. I've had to come up the hard way. Ask anybody round Owen Avenue. Sometimes I feel like I've been battered more times than a load of chip-shop haddock. Every day I'm carrying this burden on my back, you see. The dad from hell, that's who I got saddled with. A real liability. That's right, I've got a father the way some people have zits. He did a runner three years ago. Then he turns up again without so much as an apology. He's a hard man for one of the local villains, a low-life by the name of Lee Ramage. To make things worse there's a younger brother, Brain Damage Ramage, and he just has to go to the same school as me, doesn't he? We're sworn enemies.

Everybody has me down for a scally like my dad, but I'm not going to go the same way as him. Don't get me wrong, I love him in spite of everything. I just don't want to go down the same road. I'm better than that. The moment life starts to hurt, the moment I feel the pressure, that's when I come alive. Take Brain Damage, for instance. He got a bit big for his boots so I brought him down to earth. Oh, I knew he'd be back sometime, but at the time of the events in this story, he was lying low, licking his wounds.

I'm different to a lot of the lads I know. Life isn't something that happens to me. I don't just sit and take it. I grit my teeth and fight back. I'm the Guv'nor. I see the difference in every match I play with my team, the Rough Diamonds. I mean, I've had my share of troubles, so everybody thinks I'm just another two-bit scally. That's where the football comes in. On the pitch I just come alive. I start to run things. That's why they call me the Guv'nor.

Sure, there are better players. Technically, anyway. Our striker Dave Lafferty, for instance. I mean, his feet must have been kissed by the angels the way he plays! The lad's got the gift. Me, I'm a grafter. No, that's not it exactly. I'm more than that. I'm the team captain, the Guv'nor. It's like being a puppeteer. You've got to know which strings to pull. And do I know the strings!

The day I started playing for the Diamonds they were nothing. Worse than nothing; they were a joke. Rooted to the bottom of the South Sefton league and carrying the worst manager in the County FA, a pudding called Bobby Jones. That's when I started to make things happen. For a start we ditched old BJ. 'It's him or me,' he squeals one time, jabbing a podgy finger at me. And you know what, the lads chose me. So that's it, isn't it? The pressure's on. I've got my way, now it's up to me to deliver. That's what I mean by the pain barrier. Like when you go for a fifty-fifty ball. Somebody's going to blink, and it isn't me. Ever. Backing off just isn't in my nature.

Everybody's looking to me to set an example, and that's exactly what I do. Before you know it, I've led the boys to their first victory, four-three in the Challenge Cup. What a feeling! The season was nearly half over by then, and not a win to show for it. Suddenly we're playing with pride and determination. They'd been on the floor so long they thought they were worms or something. Only fit for treading on. But I changed all that. That's why I love the game, I suppose. It's a battle with winners and losers, and if you're going to win you've got to find that little bit of steel inside yourself. Only I'm going to do more than that. I already know what I've got inside me. There's steel and there's fire. That's what makes me the Guv'nor. It's what's inside the others that matters now. If we're going to start to win and win regularly, I can't do it on my own. I need a team around me.

That means me changing the lads.

Which is where this story starts. With as unlikely a pair of stars as you're going to meet. First there's Ratso. That's Pete Ratcliffe. I tell you, if you grow up in an area like the Diamond estate, you don't have too many choices. You can be tough, and in this end of north Liverpool we're talking rock hard. That's one option. Every time life knocks you down, you just bounce back up and give it a thick lip. Or you can do what Ratso does. You play the clown. Every gang's got one, a joker. Somebody who acts the fool, knocks themselves down before anybody else can do it to them. Not very promising material in a side, a kid like Ratso. Well, what do you do with somebody who's actually happy sitting out most of the season on the sub's bench and goofing it up in the changing room? Where's the aggression, the will to win? Where do you find the steel in somebody like that? We'd done well to actually get Ratso off the bench and into the side, but there was an awful long way to go. He just didn't take himself seriously.

But if Ratso's hard work, you should try having Gordon Jones in your team. Gord's got everything against him. For a start, he just isn't one of us. He's off the posh estate and that lame-brain manager we used to have, Bobby Jones, that's Gord's dad. The Joneses have a nice new detached house up on Mersey Park, overlooking the Diamond. And in front of the nice new house is a nice new car. But is Bobby Jones satisfied with a nice new house and a nice new car? No way. He has to come down the Diamond, slumming it, doing charitable works for us, the Great Unwashed. That's what really got our backs up, the way he looked down his nose at us. Like we were nothing. You know what, somebody like that would wipe their feet on your soul, and never even give you a second look. So Gord's

*got all that to live down. Which probably explains the way
he is. I mean, he's pathetic. Spineless. The original invert-
ebrate kid. (Ratso told me that one. Dead clever, Ratso.
Swallowed a dictionary with his mother's milk.)*

*Gord's been under the thumb so long, he's got fingerprints
on his head. He's a big lad, built like the Albert Dock, but he
never uses his size. He's too rotten soft. That's what comes
of being wrapped in cotton wool for eleven years.*

*And that's the challenge. How to turn the likes of Ratso
and Gord into a team. You think I've bitten off more than I
can chew? Like I said before, with a team like the Diamonds
you've got to start at the pain barrier.*

Two

Gord was watching the game with Blessed Hearts from
the subs' bench. Only it wasn't a bench, just the cool-
box where Ronnie Mintoe kept the refreshments. Gord
found himself tracking the new manager as he paced the
touch-line. A more different man to his father would
have been hard to imagine. Lean and wiry, with short,
silvery-grey hair, Ronnie was quiet and intense. If he
had nothing to say, his mouth stayed firmly shut. His
idea was to let the Diamonds do their talking the only
way they knew how – with their footy boots. What's
more, he cared about the boys. Gord hugged his
stomach as if he was in pain. To his dad the team had
never been more than a bit of charity work, a gang of
kids to boss about. Whereas Ronnie Mintoe was part of
his team, Bobby had always been detached, a superior
being. There might only be a big creosote fence
separating Mersey Park up on the hill from the

sprawling Diamond estate below, but it may as well have been the Great Wall of China.

'Think yourself lucky,' Gord's dad used to tell him, 'that you don't have to grow up in that dump. No son of mine wastes his life hanging round on street corners.'

Hardly a day went by without Gord being reminded of his advantages in life. Just one thing nagged at his dad. He'd been ditched as manager by a bunch of no-hopers from *that estate*. It was more than an upwardly-mobile deputy assistant manager in tele-sales could take. It was like coming second in a slimming contest – to Mr Blobby. Talk about wounded pride. Gord had had to beg and plead before he'd been allowed to stay in the team. His dad hadn't half gone on. 'No son of mine plays with a shower like that if he can help it.' But Gord wanted to play with a shower like that. More than anything.

'Hey, Gord,' came a reedy voice. 'Keep an eye on my ghetto-blaster, will you?'

Gord smiled at Ratso, grateful for the attention. The lads had hardly acknowledged his existence that Sunday morning. 'Sure, no problem.'

'What did *he* want, the Ratcliffe boy?'

Gord winced. His dad was back from sounding off to John O'Hara's dad about the proper way to run a team. His way.

'He asked me to watch this for him.'

'So what did his last servant die of? They're using you, son.'

Gord looked away, his eyes prickling with frustration. He just wanted to be left alone for once. But he didn't tell his dad that. He didn't dare. On the field the game was underway, and the Diamonds were under the cosh. Ronnie Mintoe's nephew Jimmy made a tackle in the box. It looked good to Gord, but the ref blew anyway. Penalty.

'Come off it, ref,' complained Ronnie. 'That was a good tackle.'

'That's right,' said Gord, faltering under his dad's withering glare. 'He played the ball.'

'Still a penalty,' his dad observed. He was enjoying the Diamonds' discomfort.

Gord said a prayer to the All-Saving God of Goalies in the great Goodison Park in the sky, but it was a well-taken penalty kick. Daz Kemble could only palm it into his own net. They were one-nil down. He glanced across at his dad.

'Something wrong?' came the frosty challenge.

'No, Dad,' said Gord, lowering his eyes. 'Nothing wrong.'

His Dad wasn't allowed to gloat for long. Dave Lafferty put the Diamonds back on terms with a rasping volley, the sort that would be in every TV compilation. If junior football was on telly, that is!

'Well,' said Ronnie turning to Gord's dad. 'Credit where credit's due, Bobby. That was good finishing.'

Bobby just grunted, and if Dave Lafferty's strike had put him in a bad mood, the next goal plunged him into deep depression. He hated Kev McGovern, and there was the Guv lurking at the far post to stab the ball in from close range.

'Goal!'

All of a sudden everybody was leaping about, fists punching the air. Not Bobby. He just stood there with a sour face. Like he'd been munching lemons.

'Oh, come on, Dad,' Gord ventured. 'Lighten up. We're winning, aren't we? We'll be through to the quarter finals of the Challenge Cup.'

'There's a long way to go yet.'

Gord's head sagged. He was dying to cheer the Diamonds on, but he couldn't forget his dad, brooding, resentful, putting a dampener on everything. That's the way he was. He crushed the life out of you.

'There's the whistle,' said Ronnie Mintoe. 'Up you get, boys. Let's sort the refreshments.'

Gord and Carl, the other sub, stood up so Ronnie could get the orange out of the cool-box.

'Going well, isn't it, Ronnie?' asked Gord. He felt it was a brave thing to do in front of his dad. Like siding with the enemy.

The second half had hardly begun when the Diamonds let Blessed Hearts back into the game.

'Soft goal,' muttered Carl. Gord nodded grimly.

Ronnie Mintoe was more vocal in his dismay. 'Oh, for crying out loud. That was your ball, Mattie. Close them down. Keep tight on your man.'

Only that morning, Mattie couldn't have kept tight on a tortoise with a wooden leg. Less than a minute later he was beaten again. The Diamonds were three-two down.

'Told you,' said Gord's dad.

Get stuffed.

Only Gord didn't say it to his face. Just, 'That was Mattie's fault again.'

Ronnie agreed. 'Gordon,' he said, 'Get your trackie off. You're on instead of Matt.'

Gord noticed the venomous expression on Carl Bain's face. 'Me?'

'That's right,' said Ronnie. 'Why, don't you want a game?'

'What's going on, Ronnie?' Carl demanded irritably. 'That wally's never been much cop. Why him?'

'Team selection's my job,' said Ronnie in a prickly

voice Gord barely recognized. 'The only thing wrong with his football was that he was played out of position.'

'Oh yeah,' sneered Carl.

Ronnie ignored him and turned to Gord. 'Listen, son. I think your dad made a mistake playing you as a striker, but I reckon you can do a job for us at the back. You've shown me what you can do on our little training sessions at the Community Centre. Now it's time to do it on the pitch. You're big enough. The question is, are you up for it?'

Gord didn't need to answer. Instead, he started peeling off his track suit while Carl nursed the humiliation of being passed over.

'Come on, Mattie. You're off, son.'

Gord's heart was beating. No, hammering, pounding out a war chant on his Adam's Apple.

'Why me?' Mattie was protesting.

'Get a move on, Matt,' said Ronnie firmly. 'Now.'

Mattie stalked to the touch-line. 'You mean you're putting soft lad on instead of me?'

Gord couldn't even look Mattie in the eye. He could barely breathe. As he ran on he could feel the other boys' eyes on him. Carl and Mattie especially, but not just them. All those eyes burning into him like lasers. They hadn't forgotten the wasted games he'd played as the league's most ill-suited centre forward, foisted on the team by his dad.

It was time to put things right.

'So where are you going to play the plank, Ronnie?' asked Guv.

Ronnie ignored the word *plank*. 'In Mattie's place.'

Guv frowned, then nodded to Ant. 'Looks like you've got a new partner.'

'Gee thanks,' grumbled Ant, 'Another passenger. Let

us down,' he warned Gord as he slotted in as a central defender, 'and I'll burst you.'

Gord could feel his eyes stinging. He felt alone and exposed. And scared of Ant.

'I mean it,' Ant continued, spitting noisily on the turf. 'I don't know what Ronnie's playing at, lumbering me with you, but one cock-up and you're dead.'

Gord nodded nervously and said another silent prayer to the Great God of Footballers. No cock-ups. *Please.* Then he heard a shout. It was Guv.

'Gord,' he was yelling angrily. 'Wake up. Watch Costello.'

'Got him, Guv,' came the stammered reply. His first test had arrived before he had time to catch his breath.

Costello was Blessed Hearts' driving force and he was bearing down on Gord. Gord watched him jinking left and right, inviting him to dive in. But Gord held off. He watched his man, following the ball, making half-turns this way and that to cover any break. Then Costello made up his mind, pushing the ball to his left. Gord felt a rush of adrenalin. This was it. He saw his chance and slid his opponent. He felt the thump of the ball on his shin. He'd done it. He'd won the ball cleanly. Cool as you like. No cock-up.

'Gord Almighty!' cried Guv disbelievingly.

'Nice one,' said Ant. His voice was a grudging snarl. 'Yeah, keep it up.' Then the barbed comment, just to show he wasn't going soft. 'If you can.'

It was about as close to praise as you got from Anthony Glover. Gord smiled inside. But it was no use looking round for any more encouragement. The ball was already up the other end of the field and the tackle was forgotten as the Diamonds pressed for the equalizer. Gord watched Dave Lafferty jog up to take a free-kick on the edge of the box. It was a stunner. Three-all.

'Come on, lads,' shouted Ratso, clapping his hands. 'We can win this one.' Then, as he passed Gord: 'That was a boss tackle, Gordon lad. Kept us in the game.'

Suddenly Gord wasn't just smiling inside. He was beaming! The feeling didn't last long. He spotted Mattie and Carl bending Ratso's ear from the touchline. Gord knew what they'd be saying. What was Ratso doing talking to Gordon the moron? Had he forgotten whose side he was on? Then the Blessed Hearts' skipper Costello sobered Gord up good style. He'd got away from Ant on the right. The speed of the attack had split the Diamonds' defence wide open, and Costello was about to go round Daz. With the goalie beaten, he would be left with a simple tap-in. That's when Gord reacted. A goal just before the final whistle would ruin everything. Nobody would remember his tackle if they lost.

'Hunnh!' Gord gave a loud grunt as he threw out his leg.

With relief, he saw the ball holding up in the muddy goalmouth. Commit himself and he was bound to make contact. The trouble was, at full stretch he would have no control over where it went.

Another word to the God of Footballers. Please.

Gord hit it with the outside of his boot. Not an own goal. Pllleeease.

He rolled on to his side and watched it trickling away. Past the outside of the post and away for a corner. He'd cleared it. There was a moment's silence. Then people were calling his name. 'Gord Almighty!' they were roaring. Even his dad looked happy.

'Amazing,' said Ratso. 'Truly amazing.'

Only Carl and Mattie cast a cloud over the

celebrations. They just stood on the line, arms stubbornly folded. For once, Gord didn't let the hostile looks get to him. The Diamonds had the opposition rocking and he'd played his part in turning the game.

'We've got them on the run,' said Guv. It was like he was everywhere, defending, attacking, urging his team mates on. The perfect captain.

'It's got to go in,' said Ant as Blessed Hearts scrambled the ball clear. 'It's *got* to.'

Just when it looked as if Blessed Hearts were going to hang on for an undeserved draw, Guv scored from a seemingly impossible angle. Gord winced. His dad wasn't going to be very pleased. He watched Guv peel away from the knot of team mates who'd been mobbing him. He was wearing a smile the size of the Mersey tunnel. He tore the shirt off his back and headed for the spectators. That's when Gord realized what was coming. Guv came face to face with the old man. He'd taken a lot from Gord's dad. Written off as a complete waste of space, accused of thieving and all sorts. Now he was getting his own back. He stood there, waving his shirt in joyful defiance. He wanted the old man to eat dirt. Dad went as red as a Liverpool shirt.

'Thanks a million, Guv,' Gord muttered under his breath. 'That's really going to help my chances of staying in the side.'

Dad would be even more determined to get him away from the Diamonds after *that* little display.

The moment the whistle went, the players formed an excited huddle on the touch-line. Aware of his dad's disapproving glare and the hostile snarls of Carl and Mattie, Gord hung around uneasily at the back of the crowd.

'We were brilliant,' said Ant.

'Guv was,' said Jimmy Mintoe.

'Don't forget Dave,' said Jamie Moore.

'And what about Bashir's crosses? How come he's kept so quiet about that left foot of his?'

Then Guv chipped in. 'Don't forget Gord,' he said. 'Those two tackles of his kept us in the game. I tell you, Gord, you could have knocked me over with a feather. I had you down as a space cadet.'

Guv was nothing if not direct.

'So I'm not a *total* space cadet, then?' he inquired.

Guv eyed him severely. Don't push it, lad!

Ratso turned and was about to give Gord an appreciative smile. Then he saw Carl and Mattie giving him daggers. Gord sighed. He had a lot of ground to make up if he was going to be accepted, but he'd made a start.

'That's it for this year, boys,' said Ronnie finally. 'No matches until the New Year. At least we finished the old one on a winning note. You've started to play to your potential. I'll see you all in the first week of January. Have a good Christmas.'

'Yes, you too, Ronnie,' the boys chorused. And they meant it. Ronnie was starting to turn the team round. Maybe they wouldn't be propping up the table much longer.

'Hey, Guv,' said Ratso as he picked up his ghetto-blaster. 'Fancy coming to McDonald's with us? There's a crowd of us. Joey, Carl, Daz, Mattie. We'll have a good laugh.'

'You'll have to count me out this time,' said Guv. 'Me, Mum and our Gareth are going swimming. Maybe next week.'

'Fair enough,' said Ratso. 'What about you, Gord?'

Carl and Mattie looked appalled at the invitation, but that's not what stopped Gord. He looked at his dad. More in hope than anticipation.

'Sorry, boys,' came the answer. 'Gordon's got homework to do.'

'It's only spellings,' said Gordon weakly.

'Nice try,' said Dad. 'But no son of mine skips his homework. Besides, we've got to call in at your nan's. Maybe some other time.'

Oh yeah, thought Gord, I bet. 'But Dad ...'

'But Dad nothing. Say goodbye, Gordon.'

Gord lowered his eyes. 'See you, lads.'

'See you,' said Ratso.

'Yes, see you,' said Daz.

Carl and Mattie didn't answer.

As Gord trailed after his dad, he bit his lip. Pressure, that's all he got.

Pressure.

Three

'What's the matter with you, anyway?' demanded Mattie, wagging a finger in Ratso's face.

Ratso shrank back. 'How do you mean?'

'Sucking up to his Lordship, that's what I mean.'

'Oh, you mean Gord.'

'That's right, Gordon flaming Jones, the Marks and Spencer Kid. Forgotten how his old man treated us, have you?'

'No,' said Ratso. 'Of course not.'

Carl snorted. 'So what makes you think we want that dipstick tagging along?'

'Nothing, I—'

'Forgetting who your mates are, Ratso?' asked Mattie. 'We go back years. That stuck up snob's just nicked my place in the team, you know.'

'Mine too,' added Carl.

'Leave him alone,' said Daz.

Ratso was grateful for the intervention. He envied Daz. He was tough. He even stood up to Guv. Sometimes.

'Well, look who's here,' said Joey Bannen.

Some of the Blessed Hearts team were straggling along County Road. They were on the other side, and they didn't look happy. Not one bit.

'Hey,' Joey chirped at the top of his squeaky voice. 'Anybody heard the footy scores?'

'Not half,' said Daz, cottoning on quickly, 'Match of the Day. Rough Diamonds four, Blessed Hearts three.'

'Get away,' said Mattie. 'Must have been a good game.'

'The best,' said Daz, his face wrinkling with a mischievous grin. 'Just the best.'

The boys were shrieking with laughter at the opposition's expense, when Ratso noticed movement. 'Hang on,' he said, his voice breaking. 'We're outnumbered here.'

They were, too, and not just by the Blessed Hearts team. The opposition seemed to have collected a few of their older brothers along the way. Ratso clocked the scally uniform; baggy Mizuna tops, Puma King jackets and trouble on their minds. What's more, they'd started to cross the road.

'Leg it!' yelled Daz.

The rest of the gang didn't need telling twice. The traffic had held Blessed Hearts up in the middle of the road, so they had a head start.

'This way,' hissed Joey as they turned into Spellow Lane.

The boys crowded into a filthy back alley and held their breath. Ratso took a chance and glanced out. 'It's

OK,' he said, 'They've lost us. They're carrying on down County Road.'

'Give them five minutes to clear off,' said Mattie. 'Then we'll nip into McDonald's.'

'Are you sure that's such a good idea?' asked Ratso. 'I mean, what if they come back? We'll be sitting ducks.'

'Oh, give over whining,' said Mattie. When it came to street cred, he thought he'd invented the manual.

'Who was the one with the big gob, anyway?' asked Ratso, doing his best not to whine. He was still sore over Gord, and wanted to have a dig at his mates over something. 'Who's the bright spark who goes winding them up when they're mob-handed?'

'Joey,' said Daz, dead loyal. 'But we all joined in, remember.'

Ratso dug his hands in his pockets and stamped away. The others followed, exchanging glances. What had gotten into him?

'Coast's clear,' said Daz.

'Right,' said Joey. 'Mine's a Big Mac.'

'I'm famished,' said Ratso. 'I'm going to enjoy this.'

Only he didn't. Not for long. Carl and Mattie had got a bee in their bonnet over Gord.

'We're going to have him,' said Mattie.

'What's he done to you?' asked Ratso.

'Stuck-up little toe-rag,' said Carl, by way of an answer. 'He needs sorting. Two jammy tackles and everybody thinks he can play. Especially him. We're going to make sure he never comes near the team again.'

'What, do him over?' asked Joey.

'Yes, why not?' said Carl.

'It won't be easy,' said Mattie. 'You never see him on his own. He's like that kid on the telly. Lives in a plastic bubble. It'll take something really clever to get him away from his mum and dad.'

Daz laughed out loud. 'Clever? Come off it, Mattie. You haven't got two brain cells to rub together. I'm off.'

He bolted the last of his fries and slugged his Coke. He was no mate of Gord's, but he didn't fancy being dragged into the middle of some stupid feud either. 'Coming, Joey?'

Joey popped in a chicken nugget. 'Yes, I'm on my way.'

Mattie watched them leave. 'So what's got into Daz?' he grumbled.

Ratso knew exactly what had got into Daz. Conscience. He wasn't the sort of lad to make somebody else's life a misery. So what's wrong with me, thought Ratso? Why don't I tell them where to get off, too? But it had taken him years to be accepted as part of the gang, an insider, and he wanted to stay part of it.

He was skinny and pinch-faced and his voice sounded like a rusty door-hinge, marginally less high-pitched than Squeaky Bannen. He only kept in with the others because he was willing to be a butt of their jokes, the clown. It was the same with the ghetto-blaster. He'd made the job his own. A new anthem for every match.

'You're the key to my plan,' said Mattie, dismissing Daz's retort. 'I think he likes you. String him along. Get him to trust you.'

'Why?' asked Ratso. 'What are you up to?'

'Ah,' said Mattie. 'That'd be telling.'

'But—'

Ratso never got to register his objection. At that very moment Carl's jaw dropped open, spilling meat and sesame bun all over his leg.

'Hey, you dirty beggar!' protested Ratso.

'Blessed Hearts,' said Carl.

— 18 —

'What?'

His words were muffled by what was left of the burger. 'Blessed rotten Hearts. There.'

He was right. They had their noses pressed against the front window and they were leering triumphantly. Costello led a raiding party inside.

'Move!' barked Mattie.

'Where?'

'Hey, mate,' shouted Mattie to one of the staff behind the counter. 'Got another door?'

'Yes. Fire exit, but you can't use it.'

The boys weren't about to stand around arguing the toss. They were over the counter and running between the chip-friers.

'Hey, you kids!'

Ratso hit the bar on the emergency door. In the time it takes to blink they were out and on their toes.

'Are they following?' panted Ratso as they reached the Brick House.

'I don't think so,' Carl replied. 'Looks like we got away with it.'

They slowed to a walk.

'So are you in?' asked Mattie.

'In for what?'

'Settling scores with Gord Almighty, that's what.'

'I don't know,' said Ratso doubtfully. 'He's never done me any harm.'

They were crossing Walton flyover by the underpass.

'Come on,' said Carl. 'Climb down off the fence. Are you with us or against us?'

Before Ratso got the chance to answer, he heard the sound of running feet. 'Oh heck, it's them again.'

Blessed Hearts hadn't given up, after all. They'd been stalking the trio from a distance.

'This way,' said Mattie. 'Oh sugar!'

Sugar was right. Members of Costello's gang were spilling out of both the left side and right side subways.

'They've done a flanker on us,' said Carl.

'So what do we do now?' cried Ratso. There was panic in his voice.

'There's only one way out,' said Mattie.

'Where?'

'There, of course.' Mattie was pointing up the steep banking that led to one of the busiest roundabouts in Liverpool.

'We're never going to cross that!'

'It's either that,' said Mattie. 'Or them.'

Ratso glanced at Costello. The fire looked marginally more inviting than the frying pan. 'OK, let's go.'

Next second he was scrambling up the concrete slope after his mates. It wasn't easy, especially hugging his precious ghetto-blaster.

'You're crazy,' he wheezed as they reached the low wall between the central reservation and the road itself. The traffic was speeding round them. The roar was in Ratso's ears and the smell was in his throat.

'Wait for the break,' said Mattie.

'What flipping break?' demanded Carl. Two lines of cars and lorries were sweeping past. It was more like Brand's Hatch than Walton.

'This one,' declared Mattie, launching himself off the wall and into the road.

'Oh well,' groaned Ratso. 'Here goes nothing.'

They made it to the pavement, but not without half a dozen drivers yelling and blaring their horns like crazy. Costello was on the wall, shaking his fist. Even Blessed Hearts weren't daft enough to follow.

'Come near our turf again,' yelled Costello. 'And you go home in a box.'

'You know your trouble?' shouted Mattie. 'You're just a sore loser.'

Ratso's heart was still hammering.

'Well,' said Mattie. 'Made your mind up yet?'

Ratso glanced at him.

'I saved your bacon, you know.'

Ratso winced. So that's what he called dragging him across the busiest road for miles.

'OK,' sighed Ratso wearily. 'I'm in.'

Four

I suppose you're thinking Ratso was weak. Well, so he was. I can understand him though. I didn't always fit in. Like when I came to live on the Diamond. People heard stuff about me, things I'd done. Bad things, the sort of things you do when you're feeling rotten and you want to hit back at the world. So I got sent to Coventry, thanks to Brain Damage. Nobody would talk to me. That's what Ratso was scared of, you see. Being alone. He was always a bit out of the ordinary. Funny-looking. Clever, though. But who needs brains when you want to be part of the gang? Brains are for nerds, teacher's pets. Kids like Ratso and kids like Gord.

So Ratso went along with Mattie. It must have made him sick to his stomach, of course. He's not a bad lad, our Ratso. Just a bit unhappy. Always wants people telling him what a great guy he is. Of course, if I'd known what they were up to, I'd have had a word. A team's a fragile balance, and I didn't need Mattie Hughes and Carl Bain breaking up the first defensive unit that looked like working. But I didn't know what was going on, and neither did poor Gord.

Yet.

Five

Coming up the street, Ratso was playing Good Day, Bad Day. It was the sort of thing he played when he was on his own, mind games. At least I've got a mind to play with, he thought, not like some. Some included Mattie and Carl just then. But they were his mates, so he had to go along with them.

Beating Blessed Hearts – Good Day.

Getting caught in McDonald's – Bad Day.

Escaping from McDonald's – Good Day.

Getting caught at the Flyover – Bad Day.

Crossing the road in one piece – Definitely Good Day (his heart was still doing the Lambada across his rib cage at the thought of it).

Agreeing to set up Gord – Bad Day, **Bad Day**, BAD DAY.

Ratso just couldn't understand what Gord had done that was so terrible. Why couldn't Carl and Mattie leave him alone? Sure, Bobby Jones was a jerk, but since when did you get marked on what your parents got up to? Why couldn't people just go with the flow? That was Ratso's style. You could get round any problem, just as long as you didn't expect everything to go your own way. And nothing ever quite went Ratso's way.

'Been having fun?' said a man's voice. The question was heavy with sarcasm.

Ratso sucked in a great lungful of air. It was Franny.

'I said,' Franny repeated. 'Have you been enjoying yourself on that roundabout?'

'Come again?' How did Franny know about the kamikaze dash across Walton roundabout?

Franny was leaning on the bonnet of his battered VW, arms folded arrogantly across his fleshy chest.

'Don't come the innocent with me, sunshine. I nearly ran you over. What do you think you were playing at?'

'Squash the Ratso?' He'd meant it to be funny, but it came out cheeky.

Franny was off the bonnet like a shot. 'Cocky little sod.'

Ratso backed off as Franny shoved his big, strawberry nose into his face.

'If I ever catch you playing there again, I'll—'

And that's when Ratso stopped playing the fool. Even a clown can lose his rag occasionally.

'You'll what? You're not even my dad.'

Which is when Franny hit him. A swinging, flat-handed clout across the temple that made him reel.

'Ow!'

'And here's another for good luck.'

The tattoed arm swung at him but this time Ratso got his hands up and the blow glanced off his raised forearms.

'Get off! Where's my mum?'

'She's making a coffee. She's just got in from work. Now get through that door. You're grounded.'

Ratso scurried ahead of Franny into the house, tucking in his behind to avoid a kick up the pants. Unfortunately for Ratso, his entrance coincided with his mum's arrival from the kitchen, carrying a couple of steaming mugs.

'Watch the coffee!' she shouted. She'd been on duty at the petrol station on the East Lancs since seven o'clock and she looked tired.

Ratso contorted his body to avoid a collision.

'The state of you,' his mum scolded. 'You look like a flaming limbo dancer. What's the matter?'

'He hit me.' Gord pointed accusingly at Franny.

Not that he expected his mum to do anything. Since

she copped off with him at the Social Club, Franny couldn't do anything wrong. It was Franny this and Franny that. You'd think he was Keanu Reeves or something, not some slob of a dwarf from Everton Valley.

'Did you?' she asked Franny.

'Too right I did,' he replied. 'Stupid little blurt nearly got himself killed. Playing chicken on Walton roundabout.'

'Oh, Peter!'

'I never, Mum, he's lying.'

'So tell me you weren't running all over the road with your stupid mates.'

Mum gave him her dismayed look. 'Peter?'

'It was these lads,' Ratso explained. 'They were chasing us. They'd have battered us, really battered us.'

'Better than getting yourself run over,' snapped Franny.

'Franny's right, love,' said Mum. 'We get plagued by kids at the filling station. They're always making a nuisance of themselves. I didn't expect one of my own sons to start acting like those young scalawags. Go to your room.'

'But Mum.'

'Up those stairs,' ordered Franny.

Ratso gave his mum a despairing glance. Tell him, he was pleading silently, tell him he's got no right to shove me around. Tell him he's not my dad. But Mum just nodded in agreement with Franny. With a long sigh, Ratso plodded upstairs.

He was allowed downstairs as the last notes of the *East Enders* theme tune drifted up from the living room. The moment he entered, his stomach clenched. Another row.

'What now?' he whispered to Aaron.

'Jason.'

'Jason. Why, what's he done?'

'He hasn't done anything. They've told him to babysit tonight.'

'How come?' Ratso asked. 'We can take care of ourselves.'

Ratso looked at his brothers. At fifteen, Jason was the oldest, followed by himself, eleven, Aaron, eight, and Dale, six. Mum had always wanted a girl, but the boys just kept arriving. Like bad pennies. Trouble times four, she would say, but that's when she used to talk to them. Since Franny moved his sweaty socks in, he was the only one who seemed to matter.

Aaron shifted along the worn couch to let Ratso sit down. 'Franny says Jason's got to stay in with us, and Mum agrees with him ...'

'Doesn't she always?'

Aaron nodded grimly. 'Jason's going mad over it. He's supposed to be going out with Tracey.'

Tracey. She was Jason's latest. The one with the nearly-crossed eyes. The one who wore flowery dresses and Doc Martens. The one who was almost pretty in an ugly sort of way. The one Ratso had a sort of crush on. Aaron said he was one sad case. Jason would have said he was a sleazebag if he'd known, but he didn't.

They heard Franny's voice from the kitchen. 'Don't you walk away from me, Jason.'

Then it was Jason's turn. 'I'm going out, and that's all there is to it. I told you we were going out last week. It's not fair springing this on me. You can't just dump the kids on me when you feel like it.'

'I can do what I like,' retorted Franny. 'And I'll thank you to lower your voice. You're not talking to your divvy mates now, you know.'

Jason appeared in the doorway. 'Moron,' he said, and he wasn't talking about one of his brothers.

Franny stormed after him. 'What was that?'

Jason's face twitched. 'Nothing.'

'I heard what you said.'

Jason turned and looked Franny in the eyes. Franny had forearms like a normal person's thighs, and fists to match, but Jason wasn't about to whine at his feet like a beaten dog.

'Then what are you asking me for?'

Franny's jaw was jutting out. 'I just want you to repeat it. Go on, say it again.'

'What, and give you an excuse to thump me? Do you think I'm stupid?'

'You must think I am,' raged Franny.

'You said it,' Jason replied icily.

Ratso smiled approvingly. That's my big brother.

At that point enter Mum, stage right. She was in a towelling bathrobe and she was still dripping from the shower. 'Who's bawling the house down?' she demanded. 'I've been at work all day, you know. Can't I even get in the shower without you starting?'

'*I* didn't start it,' said Jason.

Mum dabbed at her hair with a towel. 'If it's going to start a civil war,' she said, 'I'd rather just leave it, Fran.'

'You've got to be joking,' said Franny. 'I've got tickets for the club.'

'They didn't cost that much.'

Franny half-turned. 'So what do you want to do then, She? Stay at home all Christmas? A bundle of fun that'll be with Dozey, Dopey, Mick and Titch here.'

The brothers didn't appreciate the last bit. Dale especially hated being called Titch. They didn't like Franny calling Mum *She* like that either. It was altogether too familiar, something only their real dad was allowed to call her. But he was gone, and greasy old Franny was firmly installed in his place.

'Her name's Sheila,' said Ratso.

'You what?' asked Franny.

'Mum's name, it's not She it's Sheila.' Ratso begrudged the way Franny talked to her, the way he got her to dress in clothes a size too small for her, the way he put his arms round her waist from behind, the way the pair of them giggled in the living room after lights out. Like overgrown schoolies. It was awful. It had all happened so suddenly. One minute everything was great, then Dad did something that made Mum cry and within weeks he was gone. A few months later Franny moved in.

'You want to control these lads,' said Franny.

Mum nodded feebly. 'I do my best, Fran.'

'They need firm handling,' said Franny, 'Or they'll end up walking all over you.'

'It's a man they need,' said Mum.

Ratso and Aaron made puking gestures. If *Mein Pigface* was her idea of a man she must be hard up!

'Listen,' said Franny, pulling a fiver from his pocket. 'Go and get a video from that shop on South Parade. I'll even let you have that Tracey girl round.'

Jason hesitated.

'It's the best offer you'll get,' said Franny. 'Because if you take one step outside this house to do anything else, you'll have me to answer to.'

Jason knew when to retreat. He took the fiver.

'I'll get a couple of films,' he said. It was his way of saying the argument was a score draw really.

'There you go, She,' said Franny. 'You've got to show them who's boss.'

'Anyway,' said Mum, 'I'll finish drying my hair.' Her voice was flat. She might be taken with Franny, but she still didn't like being lectured over her kids.

'You do that, sweet thing.'

Ratso and Aaron made finger-down-the-throat-gestures as Franny followed her out of the room. When Jason returned from the video shop they were still doing their Pigface impressions. Ratso was entertaining his brothers waddling round the room with a couple of cushions shoved up his jumper.

'What's up with you lot?' asked Jason. 'Gone funny in the head, or something?'

'Franny.'

'Figures. The man's a real retard.'

'He's worse than that,' said Ratso. 'He hit me before.'

'Hit you! What for?'

'He caught me running across Walton roundabout.'

'That's dead dangerous,' said Aaron admiringly.

'Dead stupid,' said Jason. 'He shouldn't go hitting you, though. Who does the greasy slob think he is?'

'Our new dad,' said Ratso. 'That's the way he acts.'

'He'll never be our dad,' said Jason. 'Never. I'd leave home before I called him that.'

Jason meant it. He and Franny were always at loggerheads.

'Did he hurt you?' asked Jason.

'That dogsbreath,' said Ratso in his best Stallone voice, 'Nah. Just a flesh wound.'

'All the same,' said Jason thoughtfully, 'he shouldn't have laid a hand on you. You ought to mention it to Dad.'

Ratso listened to Mum and Franny giggling somewhere upstairs and he hated it. It was wrong, like spitting and talking loud in a library and laughing when a funeral procession went past. Then he heard Mattie and Carl nagging him over Gord and his stomach churned. Somehow there weren't many laughs for this clown. Maybe Dad could sort something for him. Relieve the pressure.

'You know something, Jase,' he said, 'I might just do that.'

Six

Gord shifted his weight on to his left foot and peered down the street. He watched the fine drizzle sparkling in the street lamps and the grey mist bulging between the terraced houses opposite, and he heard the echoes of a thousand tellings:

'If we're ever late, don't move. We'll be there,' *and* 'Don't talk to strangers,' *and* 'If the worst comes to the worst ask the people at the club to call you a taxi. We'll pay when you get home.'

Dad was late. Gord checked his wrist-watch. Five minutes. Nothing to worry about. Not really. Only Mum and Dad were rarely late. Like never. It was a comfortable life in many ways, well-oiled and running like a precision instrument. Everything was worked out in advance. He was bussed here and bussed there. Mum and Dad ran him round everywhere, his own personal taxi service. There was always something to do, something organized. And yet, just for once, it would be nice to do those other things. The ones his parents thought so awful; play in the street, kick a ball around on waste land, get up to mischief. But that would never do. Like Dad said: 'No son of mine wastes his life hanging round on street corners.' They made sure he didn't waste a single moment, not one stupid nanosecond. They even had house meetings, just so his time would be neatly trussed up and not an instant running loose so he could 'go astray.' He could see it all now. Synchronise diaries:

* Monday – church youth club
* Tuesday – karate
* Wednesday – chess club
* Thursday – footy practice with the Diamonds
* Friday – swimming
* Saturday – Everton home games (alternate weeks)
             – natural history club (alternate weeks)
* Sunday – am, Junior League football with the Diamonds
           – pm, homework
           – evening, visiting his nan's

Gord glanced down the street. He watched the traffic lights changing to red. Still no sign of his dad. Dad! Always going on about how he used to make dens and build dams and climb trees. But could Gord? No way.

'It's not like when I was a lad,' said Dad.

'It's the traffic,' said Mum.

'And strangers,' said Dad.

'A different world,' said Mum.

Why stop there, thought Gord. What about all the other stuff? Mad cows, planes dropping out of the sky with metal fatigue, rogue asteroids, ultraviolet radiation leaking through the ozone layer. The way his parents went on, if the polar ice-cap were to melt you could be sure it would do it smack on top of him. He could just see the headline in the *Echo*: 'Boy, 11, dies in freak Mersey tidal wave.'

So just to make sure that Gord, Mum and Dad's first – and so far last-born – son got through the day without life-threatening incident, they stuck him in the car and dropped him off. To where the fun was, or at least what *they* thought was fun.

But where was Dad now? OK, so he wanted freedom, but tomorrow would do. On this dark, drizzly evening watching the long shadows of passers-by under the street lamps, Gord was looking forward to the safety of Dad's car.

That's when he heard the grind of cycle brakes behind him.

'Hi there, Gord.'

'Oh, hi, Ratso.'

'What are you up to?'

'Waiting for my dad. He's late. I've been to the Youth Club.' Gord nodded up at the sign which read: Parish Hall.

'I know. You told me all about it today.'

Gord remembered. It had come as something of a surprise. Ratso had never shown much of an interest in him before. He was always too busy hanging round Mattie and his mates. Right out of the blue Ratso had started asking what he did in the evenings. So he'd told him. What harm could it do?

'Do you want to come round ours for a bit?' asked Ratso.

'I'd better not. My dad'll kill me if I'm not here when he turns up.'

'Come on. Only for five minutes. That won't matter.'

Gord noticed Ratso glancing over his shoulder. As if he was expecting somebody.

'Sorry, Ratso, I can't.'

Ratso looked around again.

'Something up, Ratso?'

'No, why?'

'Dunno. You seem jumpy.'

Ratso grinned. 'As the princess said to the frog.'

Gord smiled indulgently, then stepped forward to the edge of the kerb. 'Here he is now.'

The car had just bumped over the bridge and was pulling up on the other side of the road. Dad lowered the window and leaned out. 'Sorry I'm late, son. Flat tyre. I must have picked up a nail.'

The smile faded from his face as he noticed Ratso. 'Hello, Peter. Don't tell me you've started going to the Youth Club.'

'No. Just hanging round. You know.'

'Yes, Peter,' said Gord's dad. 'I know all right. Say goodnight, Gordon.'

'See you, Ratso,' said Gord. 'Last day tomorrow.'

'Yes,' Ratso answered. 'Games in the morning. Disco in the afternoon. Better than work any day. I wonder what divvy they've got to play Father Christmas this year.'

Gord slid into the passenger seat and the car pulled away. 'I'll catch you in the morning, Ratso.'

Ratso waved cheerily, then lowered his hand.

'You want to steer clear of that lad,' said Dad. 'He's bad news.'

'Ratso?' said Gord. 'He's all right.'

But Gord might have thought differently if he'd looked back. Outside the Parish Hall at that very moment Ratso was being interrogated by Mattie and Carl.

'How come you didn't get him to come down the estate like we said?' asked Mattie.

'You could have done if you'd got to the Youth Club earlier,' said Carl. 'That was the plan. What's the matter with you? Are you with us over this or not?'

There was a long pause.

'Well?'

Ratso hung his head. 'You know I am.'

Seven

'On your own, Gord?'

It was Ratso. Gord just couldn't weigh it up. Right through the Juniors, Ratso had been in the other class so they hadn't come across each other much. Ratso had even joined the skitting Gord had to put up with over his dad. Suddenly the lad was all over him. He was glad of the attention, though. It was hard to make friends when your dad vetted anybody you invited home. And failed every one of them!

'Yes, it's boring in there.'

He meant the hall where the disco was thumping away.

'I don't like discos either,' said Ratso, leaning against the wall next to Gord.

A flock of Year Six girls clattered by in their party shoes. As they passed Gord and Ratso, they burst into wild laughter.

'And that's why.'

'How do you mean?'

'Kayleigh Morris. She keeps calling me Quasimodo. You know, the Hunchback of Notre Dame. Every time she comes near me.'

'You can't wait for home-time, then,' said Gord, doing his Quasi voice. 'The bells.'

'Oh, very funny.'

'Looking forward to the holiday?' asked Gord as his joke sank without trace. Make a note, he told himself, leave the funnies to Ratso in future.

'Of course. You?'

'Dunno. Me and Nosun seem to get on each other's nerves when we're stuck in the house together.'

Ratso looked puzzled. 'Nosun?'

Gord chuckled. 'It's my nickname for the old man.

You know: *No son of mine hangs round the streets. No son of mine gets a bad school report.* Nosun.'

'Oh,' said Ratso. 'Like that, is he?'

Gord gave him a sideways look. 'Forgotten what he was like as a manager?'

Ratso rolled his eyes. 'Don't remind me.'

'Well, he's the same as a dad.'

'Poor Gord.'

'Yes, poor me.'

Gord listed his grievances:

* stupid clubs every night

* about five million aunties to visit – and kiss, even when they slobbered!

* about five million uncles to visit – and tell how he was doing at school

* a whole afternoon spent writing thank-you letters for his Christmas presents, even the duff ones

* not being able to go out when he liked

* not being able to knock around with the kids he liked

'Got a blacklist, has he?' asked Ratso.

'Not half.'

'Who's on it?'

'Who isn't? Everybody in my class, everybody in our street, Guv of course ...' He took a deep breath. '... You.'

'I worked that out last night,' said Ratso. He glanced down the corridor. 'You should take no notice. Do your own thing.'

'I wish,' said Gord. 'I daren't put a foot wrong, or he'd have me out of the Diamonds. He's looking for any excuse. He'll have me trampolining instead.'

'Trampolining?

'Yes, he brought a leaflet home last night. It was the Young Entymologists the other day.'

'Oh, insects.'

Gord did a double take. 'How did you know that?'

Ratso shrugged his shoulders. 'Must have picked it up somewhere.'

He'd noticed that about Ratso. He had a brain like a vacuum cleaner. That used to annoy his dad too. Every time he'd tried to show off his football knowledge, there would be Ratso going one better.

One time Guv had sprung a quiz question on the team. 'What was the first team Bill Shankly played for?' he asked.

'Preston North End,' said his dad.

'Glenbuck Cherrypickers,' said Ratso.

No prizes for guessing who had the right answer.

'Anyway,' Ratso continued, glancing down the corridor and lowering his voice conspiratorially. 'He can't take you out of the team. Not now.'

'Why not?'

'Because you did the business against Blessed Hearts, that's why. January's a big month for us. If we can put a run together we could even get off the bottom. It won't be easy, though. Have you seen who we're up against?'

'I can't quite ...'

Ratso reeled off the fixtures. 'St Pat's, Ajax Aintree, Longmoor Celtic. All of them in the top four. We've only got one game you could call easy.'

'Tough, eh?'

'You said it. We can do it, though.'

'You reckon?'

Ratso was warming to his theme. 'I know it. Guv and Dave are really clicking up front. Bash is a talent on the wing —'

'Quick, isn't he?' interrupted Gord. He was dying for Ratso to say something complimentary about him too.

'Then there's Daz,' Ratso continued. 'He's a proper goalie. He actually likes playing between the sticks.'

'Yes.'

'So you've got to stay in the team, Gord. You did really well on Sunday.'

Gord came over all modest. 'You think so?'

'Yes, you and Ant could really click. You've just got to toughen up, that's what Guv reckons.'

Ratso hesitated and gave another of those nervous glances over Gord's shoulder.

Gord looked round but saw nothing. 'The defence couldn't get much worse, could it? How many have we let in?'

'Thirty-six,' said Ratso. 'And that's only in the league. We've conceded three more in the cup. Generous, aren't we?'

Gord nodded. 'And how many have we scored?'

Ratso had the answer to that, too. Naturally. 'Eleven in the league. Minus twenty-five goal difference. Chronic, isn't it? Still, we knocked four in in the Challenge Cup.'

'Thank you, Statto,' Gord teased.

Ratso just grinned. 'Hello, here's Jimmy. I wonder what he wants.'

He meant Jimmy Mintoe.

'Message from Uncle Ronnie,' said Jimmy. 'Training sessions have changed. Every Monday night from January.'

Monday! Gord felt sick.

'Something wrong?' asked Ratso.

'Monday?' stammered Gord. 'You did say Monday?'

'That's right,' said Jimmy. 'Uncle Ronnie's shifts have changed.'

'But that's no good to me,' Gord protested.

'Why, what's up with Mondays?'

'The Youth Club,' Gord answered. 'That stupid Youth Club.'

'Can't you drop it?' asked Jimmy. 'It's no big deal.'

'With my dad, it is,' groaned Gord. 'With him, *everything*'s a big deal.'

Jimmy shrugged his shoulders. 'Anyway, I'm going to tell Carl and Mattie.'

Gord was surprised to see him walk straight to an alcove down the corridor, from which Carl and Mattie emerged. For a moment he could have sworn that Ratso blushed, but he immediately put it to the back of his mind. He'd made a friend, and that was all that mattered.

Eight

For once Gord struck lucky. The Youth Club was closed for the first week in January so it didn't clash with training after all. Gord had another week to prepare for the showdown with his dad. Mentally, physically, emotionally, as they say in the pre-match build-up. He was just working out his moves when he heard his mum.

'Are you up there, Gordon?'

'In my room.'

'There's someone here for you.' Gord heard her talking on the doorstep. 'What's your name? I beg your pardon.'

Gord poked his head out of his bedroom window. It was Ratso.

'That can't be your real name,' Mum was saying. 'Oh, Peter. That's better.'

Better! How was it better? Give me a Ratso over a

Peter any day, thought Gord. Peters sit at home doing their homework and copying the things off *Art Attack*. But Ratsos! They go out and live. Ratsos get up to all sorts. Gord was feeling good. He had a mate, a real mate. So long as his dad didn't put the mockers on it.

'Gordon,' called Mum. 'Peter's here for you.'

Gord glanced at the clock. Dad would be home in half an hour. He'd have to work fast.

'All right, Ratso,' he said, by way of greeting.

Ratso grinned, but he looked uncomfortable. 'Coming down South Road?' he asked.

'Mum,' said Gord. 'Can I?'

'Can you what? I wasn't listening.'

'Can me and Ratso go to training by ourselves this week.'

Mum's face was a picture. She was torn between giving her son the dead eye or looking all sugar and spice for Ratso's benefit.

Couldn't be seen looking rattled in front of the Great Unwashed, could we? She ended up wearing a weird, lopsided grin, like she'd been drinking neat vinegar but wanted to keep it quiet.

'Did you mention this to your dad?' she asked, passing the buck.

'No,' said Gord. 'Forgot.'

Lame, Gord told himself, she'll never swallow that.

'Mmm.'

She didn't.

'We'll be all right,' said Ratso. 'I know my way round.'

By the look on her face, that's what Mum was afraid of. 'I'm not sure,' she said doubtfully. 'On that estate.'

'It's not so bad,' said Ratso. 'I live on the Diamond, myself. Nothing wrong with the place, so long as you know who to avoid.'

Gord made a mental note. If he wanted to be allowed out on his own, he'd have to put sticking plaster over Ratso's big mouth.

'I'll run you down,' said Mum. 'Better still, you could hang on for your dad.'

'But I've got my bike,' said Ratso.

'We've got a cycle carrier,' Mum informed him. 'I can take the pair of you *and* your bike.'

'But we'll go straight there,' said Gord. 'Won't we, Rats?'

Ratso nodded.

'And no messing about.'

Ratso nodded vigorously.

'But it will be dark by the time it finishes,' said Mum.

'Pick me up at the end if you want,' said Gord triumphantly. He was into the home straight. 'Oh, go on, Mum. You're always saying I'll have to have more independence.'

Good word, he told himself. He'd got her rocking. 'After all, I've got to go to the High School by myself in September.'

Ratso smiled. He knew a winning manoeuvre when he saw one.

'OK,' she said slowly. 'If you promise to go straight there.'

It was easy after that. All that was left was to negotiate the pre-departure briefing.

Mum: 'Don't forget your cycle helmet.'

Gord: 'No, Mum.'

Mum: 'Remember your signals.'

Gord: 'Yes, Mum.'

Mum: 'No racing.'

Gord: 'No, Mum.'

Mum: 'And no talking to strangers.'

Gord: 'Not even if they offer me a puppy.'

Mum scowled. He wasn't taking this seriously. 'And what do you do if something goes wrong?'

Gord: 'Hail a taxi.'

And that was it. He'd done it. They were out of the house and riding down the short cut behind the big, creosote fence.

'Do you have to go through that palaver every time they let you out?' asked Ratso.

'What do you mean *every* time?' asked Gord. 'This is the first time they've let me out on my own in the evening.'

'You're kidding!'

''Fraid not.'

'It must crack you up.'

Gord nodded ruefully.

'Race you,' said Ratso.

What would Mum say, thought Gord, then pedalled furiously after Ratso. What the eye doesn't see, the heart can't grieve over. Ratso won the race to South Parade, but Gord didn't care. He was free.

'You'd better take that thing off before we get to the Commo,' said Ratso.

'What?'

'That.' He meant the cycle helmet.

'Oh, right.' Bad for street cred, a wimpy helmet.

Gord tucked it into his cycle bag and followed Ratso to the Community Centre. Ronnie was already there, leaning on his car. So was Mattie Hughes. For a reason that evaded Gord, he was smiling.

'Aye aye,' came a voice. 'What's this? Mummy and Daddy started letting you out on your own?'

It was Carl.

'No harness, either,' said Mattie. 'Watch you don't get lost.'

'What happens if you're late back?' asked Carl. 'Turn into a pumpkin or something?'

Gord smiled, but he hated it.

The rest of the team had arrived by then, so Ronnie called them together. 'Right, gather round, lads,' he said. 'It's Warbreck Wanderers this Sunday. You probably remember our last meeting.'

'Six-two defeat,' said Ratso. 'First game of the season.'

'Thank you, John Motson,' said Ronnie. 'Anyway, as my fact-finding friend here has pointed out, they took us to the cleaners back in August. This is a big game for us. We got our first league point against Fix-It DIY, and last time out we got our first victory of the year in the Cup. You could say we were on a roll.'

'You could say that,' grumbled John O'Hara. 'Now we've got to prove it.'

'Well, thank you Mr Happy,' said Ronnie.

Everybody laughed.

'Mind you,' Ronnie continued, 'John's right in a way. You're a different side lately. You've got a bit of faith in yourselves, but it's no use playing good stuff if you don't get the results. The big thing we've got to concentrate on is our defence. We're a bit ...' A moment's hesitation '... porous.'

'Eh?'

'Full of holes,' Ratso explained.

'That's right,' said Ronnie. 'We're leaking goals like nobody's business. We even conceded three against Blessed Hearts. All down to defensive errors.'

Mattie bit his lip.

'So we're going to play five-a-side, and I'm not looking for goals. This is practice. One team does all the attacking, the other defends. What I want to see is a nice, tight back four.'

It wasn't easy at first. All the boys wanted to do was win, but after a few juicy rollockings from Ronnie they got the idea. Gord found himself attacking and Mattie facing him in defence. It was an unequal contest. Mattie couldn't get the ball.

'Get into him, Matt,' shouted Carl.

Mattie tried, but Gord just brushed him off.

'Good,' said Ronnie. 'Now, swop over.'

The first time Gord got in a tackle, Mattie was up, fists flailing. It was pure frustration.

'Whoa, whoa, what's all this in aid of?' asked Ronnie, stepping between them.

'Beats me,' said Gord confidently.

But nothing did beat him. He'd always been a soft touch until the game against Blessed Hearts gave him confidence. So had Ratso's friendship. He'd made a monkey out of Mattie. The place against Warbreck was his for the taking.

'Hello,' said Mattie, doing his best not to sound down, 'look who's here, Gord.'

Gord didn't need to look. Hoisting his bike on the carrier, he waved goodnight to Ratso.

'Thanks for the lift, Dad,' he said.

But he didn't mean it.

Nine

I smelt a rat, or was it a Ratso. For a start, what were him and Gord doing arriving together? A case of the odd couple. I don't go to the same school as most of the lads. I'm at Cropper Lane over by the hospital. Most of them go to Our Lady's on the far side of the Diamond by the East Lancs. That's why it came as a surprise to see them so matey all of a sudden. It felt wrong, somehow. The way Mattie and Carl were watching Gord's every move. The way they were keeping tabs on Ratso, too. I even saw Carl winking at Ratso, like they'd got this big secret. It didn't take a genius to work out the three of them were up to something. I'd come to expect it from Mattie and Carl, but I must admit I was a bit disappointed in Ratso. I didn't think he was like that. I hate it when people gang up on somebody for no reason. I've been on the receiving end of it from Brain Damage, so I've got a nose for it. Those sort of secrets give me the creeps. That's what got under my skin more than anything, the idea that they had a secret from me. I'm the captain, the Guv'nor. Nobody's supposed to keep things from me. I run the team and I run it smoothly. No aggro from anyone.

All Christmas I'd been keeping myself in shape. Christmas morning I was down the garages knocking a ball about. And with every kick I was planning Warbreck's downfall. I could see it all. Every step-over, every back-heel, every one-two. I worked the moves through in my head, over and over. I was a human video machine and there was only one tape playing. A Rough Diamonds victory and three points in the bag. And the Warbreck game was only a stepping stone to greater things. I'd got bigger fish to fry. Ajax Aintree, Longmoor Celtic, the sides who'd had the league sewn up for the last few seasons.

And was I going to let the Fun Boy Three ruin it all? I decided I would be keeping an eye on Mattie and Co. from now on. One false move and I'd sort them good style.

Nobody puts the mockers on my team.

Ten

Gord made a long clearance down the right. As Ratso shunted it on, he gave him the thumbs up – much to Mattie's annoyance. On the field Ratso was out of Mattie and Carl's clutches. Both of them were kicking their heels on the touch-line.

'Didn't know soft lad had it in him,' grunted Ant as he jogged past.

'Gord's OK,' said Ratso, and immediately felt a rush of shame. What was he doing going along with Mattie's sick scheme? 'It's not his fault his old man's a plank.'

Then it was conversation over. The Diamonds' attack had broken down on the edge of the opposition box and Warbreck were breaking fast.

'I'll try to get in a tackle,' said Ant. 'You chase that lad making the run.'

Ratso did as he was told, but there was no danger. The ball ran aimlessly out of play. As Ratso collected it, he heard a shout: 'Pete!'

'Oh, hi there, Dad.'

Ratso waved and took the throw. Seeing his dad – his real dad, not that slimeball Franny – made him feel good.

'*That's* your dad,' said Gord. 'So who's the little fat feller?'

'Oh, you must mean Franny. My step-dad. Well, step-boyfriend.'

Gord looked confused.

'That ...' Ratso pointed to the tall, dark-haired man on the touch-line. '... That's my proper dad.'

No sooner were the words out of his mouth than Dave Lafferty opened the scoring with a long, looping shot into the top left-hand corner.

Five minutes later it was two-nil. Jimmy Mintoe ran

half the length of the field before hitting it low across the Warbreck penalty area for Guv to side-foot in.

'Hey, Gord,' shouted Ratso. 'How does it feel to be on the winning side for a change?'

'We've not won yet,' said Gord, but he was grinning broadly. Mattie and Carl weren't.

Just before half-time Bashir shook off his marker and set off on one of those blistering runs of his. It didn't even matter that he got stuck in the mud down the far end, because Jamie Moore picked it up and forced it home. It was a soft, almost comic goal bobbling over the diving goalie. But who cared? The Diamonds were three-nil up and coasting.

'What's this, Pete?' asked Ratso's dad as they came off at half-time. 'I thought you always got walloped.'

'Not seen us for a bit though, have you?' Ratso replied acidly.

His dad's face clouded. 'It's been hard, son, what with the split.'

It was Ratso's turn to frown. He didn't like being reminded. The rows between his mum and dad had been terrible. And they'd erupted so suddenly. One minute it was Happy Families, the next it was Bosnia. Dad had walked out more than once. He was usually gone a couple of days before the tearful reunion. Jason reckoned it was other women, that's why Mum had taken up with Franny. Revenge. But neither Mum nor Dad had ever given a hint of what it was really about. It blew a hole in Ratso's life, though. Never in his wildest imaginings had he dreamt that Dad would actually walk out for good. Now he was living in a grotty bedsit in Orrell Park. It always smelt of onions and disappointment.

'Yes, I know.' Ratso said it kind of flat. So his dad

would feel guilty. 'I'd better listen in on Ronnie's team-talk.'

Dad nodded, but he looked annoyed.

'Something wrong?' asked Gord as he dropped to the turf to listen to Ronnie's pearls of wisdom.

Ratso shrugged.

In the event, Ronnie didn't have much to say. Just: 'Full marks on the first-half performance, lads. Keep it up.' He leant forward as if to pass on a confidence. 'Seen who's on the next pitch?'

It was Longmoor Celtic, in their green and white hoops. Last season's champions.

'Yes, Longmoor,' said Guv. 'So what?'

'They've been clocking you, that's so what. It's quite a compliment. I think you've got them worried.'

'Excellent,' said Guv. 'So let's keep them worried. Come on, lads. Let's turn on the style. My family's watching.' He waved to his mum and his kid brother, Gareth. 'Give them hell.'

The boys rose as one and headed for the pitch. But for Ratso there was no escaping Mattie.

'What's going on, eh? I thought we were going to have Little Lord Fauntleroy.'

Ratso looked away, biting his lip.

'So what are you doing about it?'

Without another word Ratso moved away. He was getting sick of Mattie.

'I haven't finished with you yet.'

Ratso spun round. He'd had enough. Gord hadn't been his mate at the start of all this, but he was now. Ratso wasn't going to play the fool any more. The team had started to do the business. Why not him? 'Well, I've finished with you, Mattie. Get somebody else to do your dirty work.'

Mattie's face was a picture. Carl's too. They just

stood there, mouths open like it was the fly-catching season.

On the pitch the Diamonds were in command. Every time Gord got the ball there was Mattie craning forward, willing him to make a pig's ear of it. But Gord was on top of his game. Nothing fancy, just good, solid tackling and simple, no-nonsense clearances. He was in his element. Ratso turned and looked across at Mattie, as if to say: *that's my mate*. His mind was made up. Come the full-time whistle he was going to let Gord know everything.

'Ratso.' He looked up. 'Rats, *Ratso*.'

It was Guv.

'Yes?'

'You can join in the attack if you want. You're hardly needed at the back.' Ratso set off upfield. 'Oh, and Ratso.'

'Yes?'

Guv had that look on his face. The soul-shrivelling glare that said he wasn't happy. 'I want a word with you after the match.'

'What about?'

'You'll find out.'

It sounded ominous. Ratso stared after Guv as he trotted away, then turned to Gord. 'I wonder what that's about? Anyway, wish me luck.'

'You won't need it,' said Gord. 'Give it some welly, Rats.'

'Push up, Ratso,' said Dave. 'We're going to batter them.'

It sounded good. Batter them. Not just beat them. *Batter* them. The Diamonds, bottom of the league, the licking boys, giving the opposition a hiding. Bashir lost his man and started a run. The ball sailed over the defenders and fell beautifully for Dave. A toe-poke and he'd netted his second.

'Four-nil,' roared Guv. 'Four flaming nil. Are you listening, Longmoor?'

Ratso looked across to the next pitch. Their manager was certainly paying attention.

After that, it was a rout. Dave got his hat trick. Then a fourth. With a couple of minutes to go Jamie got in on the act, heading it over the line from Guv's corner.

'Six.' Guv turned to the players on the neighbouring pitch. 'Got that? We're six-nil up. Watch out, the Diamonds are coming.'

The boys in the green hoops smiled indulgently. They weren't about to let on that they were worried.

Right on full time, Bashir won another corner. This time Ratso was determined to get in on the act. He went for the ball, only it went for him first. He felt a thump in the face, then a wetness then a numb feeling from his eye to his jaw.

'Somebody hit me,' he moaned. 'They rotten well hit me.'

'Don't be soft,' shouted Dave as he jumped on Ratso's back. 'You've scored.'

Ratso opened a disbelieving eye. It was true. The corner ball had smacked him in the face and rebounded into the net.

'Nice one, Rats,' said Guv, adding his congratulations. 'Pity you don't handle yourself so well off the field. Still, I'll get that sorted.'

Ratso frowned. What *was* he on about?

And that was it. The ref blew a few moments later and the Diamonds ran off the field, seven-nil victors. Ran off the field? No, they *floated*.

'I'm impressed,' said Ratso's dad. 'A bit better than the last game I saw. You got battered four-nil. Anyway,

I'm off, son. I'll pick you and the boys up later. We'll go for a pizza.'

'See you, Dad,' said Ratso. Dad was basically all right, and he really was having a hard time.

Ratso knew he still cared about Mum. He just wondered why they couldn't sort themselves out. It was one thing making each other miserable, but why take it out on the kids. Parents quarrelling, Ratso thought, there ought to be a law against it.

'Your skipper about?' came a boy's voice, breaking in on his thoughts. 'Somebody McGovern.'

'Guv?' asked Ratso. 'Yes, he's over there with his family. Why?'

The lad was wearing the green and white of Longmoor. They were worried, all right! 'He's been shouting his mouth off, that's why. You're playing us in a couple of weeks. Do you really think you can take us?'

'Of course we can,' said Ratso. 'No problem. I'll lay you any odds.'

'We might just take you up on that,' said the Longmoor player.

'Yes, you do that,' said Ratso. 'Put your money where your mouth is. I'll bet you anything you like we can beat you.'

'We'll see,' said the Longmoor boy. 'I'll be in touch.'

Ratso smiled to himself. Everything was coming up roses. The Diamonds had won, his dad had turned up and he'd sorted Mattie. Or at least he thought he had. As Ratso approached his team mates he saw Guv talking to Gord. He saw Gord stiffen, then turn in his direction. His friend's expression made his heart sink. Without a word, Gord stormed away towards Jacob's Lane, where his dad was waiting.

'Gord!' cried Ratso. 'Hang on a minute.'

Ratso started to chase after Gord, but Guv stepped

into his path, barring the way. 'I want a word with you, remember,' he said. 'I've just put Gord wise over your and Mattie's little game. I expected better of you Ratso, I really did.'

'But Guv–'

'But nothing,' Guv retorted fiercely. 'You don't do that to a mate. It's a real low-life trick. Try anything like that again and you'll have me to answer to. You and the other two.'

'What did you tell him?' groaned Ratso, watching Gord being driven away.

'The truth,' said Guv. 'That's all.'

'The truth?' repeated Ratso. 'Guv, you haven't got any idea.'

PART TWO

Pressure Building

One

I really excelled myself this time. I mean, this was like netting a sixty-yard own goal. Some Guv'nor!

I should have left well alone, had a bit of trust in somebody. Funny, isn't it? That's what I used to tell my cousin Cheryl. She's always interfering, being the do-gooder. She thinks she can turn me into a saint or something. She's tried often enough. I just wanted her to keep out of my business. Now I'm the one shoving his oar in when he's not wanted. But how was I to know Ratso had it covered? I never thought in a million years he'd have the bottle to tell Mattie where to get off. I mean, it's a wonder he can tie his own shoelaces. I thought he was a real wimpoid. I was trying to help, that's all.

Still, no excuses. I've got to hold my hands up to this one. I stuck my nose in where it wasn't wanted, and I deserve to get it chopped off. It would have been better if Ratso had popped me one, to be honest. When I found out what had really gone on, I wanted him to hit me, I really did. It would have made me feel better. I'd have given him a free shot, and I haven't done that too often.

He wasn't angry though. He didn't shout or rage or do any of the things I'd have done. He just stood there looking miserable.

'You've got to explain,' I told him. 'I'll give you a hand.'

'Oh no,' said Ratso. 'You've done enough already, thank you very much. Just keep out of it, OK?'

Then off he went. I think Mattie and Carl were going to say something, but I gave them the evil eye. They just let him go. Wise of them, don't you think?

That's about it, really. I'd tried to help and I'd only made things worse. In future I was going to steer clear until somebody asked for my help. I'd be keeping an eye on things, mind. Just in case.

Two

'Is everything all right, son?'

Gord kept his eyes firmly on the petrol pump as his dad filled the tank. He didn't want his dad to see the tears welling up.

'Fine.' He said it in a thick voice. The unmistakable sound of misery.

Dad poked his head through the open window. 'Has somebody been having a go at you? Is it that little gutter-rat McGovern?'

'No, Dad, nothing like that.'

'What then?'

'Leave it, eh?'

Dad smacked his palm down on the bonnet. 'I will not leave it. Now, either you tell me what's upset you or I turn this car round and we go straight back to Jacob's Lane.'

'No, Dad, don't!'

'I knew it. You're being bullied, aren't you? Come on, Gordon, let's have it. No son of mine gets pushed around, mark my words.'

'It isn't like that. Not really.'

'Then what is it like?'

'I've fallen out with Ratso.'

That's when his dad started laughing. 'And that's it? Honestly, Gordon, I thought it was something important.'

Gord's eyes flashed angrily. 'It *is* important.'

'You don't want to worry about a two-bit scally like Peter Ratcliffe,' snorted Dad. 'It was only a matter of time before he showed his true colours. So what's he been up to?'

Gord was watching the petrol station attendant serving a customer. He recognized her. Of all people, it had to be Ratso's mum. Ratso had told him she worked in a petrol station, but he hadn't realised which one. He just wanted his dad to keep his voice down.

'Nothing, Dad. I told you. It doesn't matter.'

'If it matters to you, then it matters to me. What did he do?'

'It was him and two other lads.'

'Which lads?'

'Mattie and Carl.'

Dad pulled a face. 'I might have guessed.'

Gord watched boys walking past in their football kits. Ajax Aintree, Fix-It, Northend United. They were something he'd felt part of. Until then.

'Ratso was never really my mate. They were pulling a trick on me.'

'Trick? What sort of trick?'

Gord felt humiliated. It would take just one *I told you so* and he would hate his dad forever. 'They set me up. Ratso only pretended to make friends, so they could get me on my own.'

Dad gave him a level stare. 'Go on, son.'

Gord took a deep breath. He knew the anger was building inside his dad. 'I think they were going to work me over.'

'I told you, son. Didn't I tell you? Scum, the lot of them on that estate. Look how they treated me. I gave up all my weekends and ...'

Gord was shaking his head.

'Now what?' asked Dad.

Gord wanted to tell him. Every time he tried to talk about his problems, Dad just started talking about himself. Like he was the centre of the universe. And he'd said it: *I told you so.* Now he really would hate his dad forever.

'Gordon?'

It was like he was a volcano and the words were the lava about to spill out. Only they didn't. There are things stronger than the truth, and fear's one of them. And Gord was definitely afraid of his dad.

'You know what?' said Dad, suddenly decisive. 'I *am* going to turn this car round. I'm going to have it out with that bunch of young thugs. And that manager of theirs.'

Gord ground his teeth. This wasn't about him any more. It was Dad's show. He was out for revenge.

'Don't, Dad.'

'And why not, may I ask?'

'Because I've still got to go to school with them. Oh, don't make it any worse. Please.'

Then his dad did make it worse, but not over the team. Mrs Ratcliffe had been watching them for a while. She opened the window of her booth. 'Is everything all right over there?' she asked.

Dad's head snapped round. 'I'd thank you not to interrupt. This is none of your business. I'm having a word with my son.'

Gord winced. Dad could be *so* embarrassing.

'Pardon me for breathing,' said Mrs Ratcliffe. 'I was only wondering if you were going to pay today, or whether you'd like me to book a hotel room while you hold your little conference.' She pointed to a queue of three cars waiting to use the pump.

'So what about the team?' asked Dad, ignoring the glares of the impatient drivers.

Gord lowered his eyes and fell silent.

'Gordon?'

He knew what Dad was asking.

'You don't need to worry about that any more, Dad. I've finished with them. For good.'

Three

'Are you off your food, son?'

It was the third time Ratso had pushed the slice of pepperoni pizza round his plate. 'What?'

'I said,' his dad replied. 'Have you gone off your food? I thought you liked pizza.'

'I'll have his,' said Aaron eagerly.

'Oh no you won't,' said Dad. 'You've not finished your own yet.'

'I will, though.' Aaron immediately started stuffing in gobbets of pizza until his cheeks bulged.

'You're disgusting,' said Jason.

Aaron didn't care. He had his eyes fixed greedily on Ratso's pizza.

'Go on. You can have it.'

Dad watched Aaron stab his fork into the pizza, then turned to Ratso.

'So what's up, Pete? Are you sick?'

He was, but not the way Dad meant. 'I'm all right.'

'OK,' said Dad. 'So you don't want to talk.'

It wasn't true. He wanted to, more than anything, but not in front of his brothers. Especially not Dale and Aaron.

'How's your mother?' asked Dad, changing the subject.

'All right,' said Jason.

'And Tracey? It is Tracey, isn't it?'

'She's all right too,' said Jason.

'Good, good.' As a conversationalist, their dad would have made a good axe murderer.

'It isn't good,' said Ratso quietly.

'Pardon?'

'At home. It isn't good. I hate it.'

'Why, what's going on?'

Ratso could feel his brothers looking at him. 'Mum's acting stupid.'

Dad raised an eyebrow. 'Now that tells me everything.'

Ratso was still preoccupied with the mess over Gord. This conversation he didn't need.

'Tell Dad about her clothes,' said Aaron.

'What about her clothes?'

'She's making herself look ridiculous,' said Jason acidly.

'Showing her belly,' said Dale.

'He means those bare midriff tops,' said Ratso.

'She's wearing those?' asked Dad. He sounded upset. Somehow Ratso had a feeling Dad didn't want to be split up at all.

'She thinks she's a rotten teenager,' said Jason.

'Come off it, Jase,' said Dad. 'She's a grown woman. She can wear what she likes.' But it was a lukewarm defence. It was who she was wearing the clothes for that seemed to be bothering him.

'No she can't,' retorted Aaron.

'Why not?'

'Because she's ...'

'She's ...'

Dale and Aaron dried up. They looked hopefully at Ratso.

'She's our mum,' he explained.

'Ah,' said Dad. 'And you want things back the way they were?'

'That's right,' said Jase. 'She's embarrassing. She's always going out.'

'She's got a right to a life,' said Dad, but this was no more convincing than anything else he'd said. Ratso examined his face. Somehow the words didn't ring true. He was no happier with the breakup than the boys.

'Anything else?' asked Dad. He tried to be funny. 'Besides her clothes?'

'*Mein Pigface*,' said Aaron bitterly.

'Oh, you mean this new feller of hers,' said Dad, a little quiver creeping into his voice. 'Whatsisname?'

Dad knew exactly what he was called. He obviously couldn't bring himself to say it.

'Franny,' said Ratso.

'Yes, that's right,' said Dad. 'Does anyone want afters by the way?'

Aaron did. And Dale. Jason was watching his figure. For Tracey. And Ratso? He was right off his food. Even blackcurrant cheesecake and cream. Dad nodded at the waitress and ordered the dessert.

'So what's wrong with this Franny character?' The way Dad said it, he clearly wanted a fine old list of defects. As long as possible.

'What's right with him, more like,' said Jason obligingly. 'He's a retard.'

'Fat,' said Dale.

'And sweaty,' said Aaron. 'He calls Mum *She* ...'

'And pats her bum,' interrupted Dale.

Dad looked uncomfortable.

'He's a slob,' said Jason. 'Thinks he can boss us

around.'

'Fair enough,' said Dad, with false good humour. 'A fat, sweaty, retarded slob. The defence rests.'

The boys didn't enjoy the attempt at humour.

'That's not all,' said Jason. 'Tell him, Pete. That's why you're not eating, isn't it? Tell Dad what he did.'

Ratso grimaced. Why did everybody have to try to help? First Guv, now Jason. And both of them way wide of the mark.

Dad was frowning. 'What did he do?'

Ratso's head sagged.

'Pete?'

'He hit me.'

'Hit you!'

Dad's eyes were hard, like stones. Ratso had seen the look before. Dad didn't lose his cool often, but when he did he went truly ballistic.

'It wasn't much.' Ratso started to backtrack. 'A clip round the ear, that's all.'

It was too late. Dad's jaw clicked, and a muscle tensed in his temple. On a temper scale of one to ten, he scored an eleven. 'I'll kill him,' he said.

'Oh Dad, don't,' pleaded Ratso. 'I wish I hadn't told you.'

But the damage was done.

Four

You never know what's going on with other people, do you? All the time I was having Dad trouble I thought nobody else ever felt like I did. People don't let on, you see. They can be having the most rotten life imaginable, but the moment you ask them how things are going what do they say: 'All right.'

You put on this act. Me, I come on like a real hard knock. Ratso plays the fool. We're the same under the skin, though. We just want what everybody else seems to have, a proper mum and dad, a good holiday to tell your mates about, a few laughs. You need people you can rely on. Instead, all you end up with is one long pain in the neck. I mean, who wants to go around apologizing for their own mum and dad? The bit I hate is when the kids start talking about their parents' jobs. My dad works at Fords, my dad's a porter. What about you, Guv? Oh, mine? He's a professional thug.

I never really knew how things were for Ratso. I suppose in a way it was worse for him than it is for me. Well, I can hardly remember what it was like with Dad at home, and after all the disappointments I suppose I know what to expect. It's that long since he walked out. There's no Golden Age to look back at. It's different with Ratso. He can remember the good times. They were only yesterday. Everything seemed hunky-dory, then the world fell in on him.

I just wonder what that does to you?

Five

'Has anybody seen Gordon?' asked Ronnie.

It was the question Ratso had hoped he wouldn't ask.

'Peter, have you seen him?'

'No.'

It wasn't true. He'd *seen* Gord, but that was about it. He'd tried to get close to him all day at school, to explain, but it would have been easier to milk a bull. Gord wasn't having any.

Ronnie sighed. If there was one thing he demanded,

it was self-discipline. He insisted that they take the team seriously. 'We'll have to start without him, then.'

Ratso leant against the chain-link fencing. He could feel the rain that had gathered on it soaking through his shirt, but he didn't care. Things were getting on top of him.

Ronnie looked at his watch. 'If he isn't here in ten minutes, he's had it for Sunday.'

'You've got to be kidding,' Guv interrupted. 'He had a cracking game for us against Warbreck. Give him a chance, eh?'

Ronnie glanced at Kev. He was a little taken aback. Until then they'd always seen eye to eye. Over the need for self-discipline, over tactics, over the style of play. The last thing he'd expected was disagreement from that quarter. 'I am giving him a chance, Kev,' he said, 'Ten minutes' worth.'

'But we need him in defence,' Guv continued undeterred. 'Tell him, Ratso.'

Ratso had nothing to say.

'Listen Kev,' said Ronnie. 'I know Gord played well. He really looked the part, but we need lads we can rely on. That means the match *and* training. No prima donnas in this team.'

Ratso envied Guv his certainty, his absolute conviction that he was right. Despite himself, Ratso had started to wonder if he should make peace with Mattie and Carl. Then he hated himself for even thinking it.

'Anyway,' said Ronnie. 'You know your groups. Passing practice.'

Ratso breathed a sigh of relief. Mattie and Carl were in a different group.

'Wake up, Rats,' shouted Guv.

Ratso looked up. 'You what?'

'The ball. I passed it to you, or didn't you notice?'

'Oh, sorry.'

Everybody laughed.

'Ground control to planet Ratso,' said Guv. 'WAKE UP!'

Guv already seemed to have forgotten he was partly to blame for this mess, but Ratso was in no mood for an argument. He nodded obediently and jogged after the ball.

'Now what are you doing?' asked Guv. 'Group passing, Rats. You're too close.'

Ratso stared back blankly.

'You help make a square round me,' Guv explained. 'The players at each point of the square pass it to me and I knock it out to the next player. Got it?'

Of course Ratso had got it. They'd done it before, loads of times. He had things on his mind: a mate he'd betrayed, a mum in the middle of her second childhood, a dad on the rampage. Stuff like that. He was under pressure.

Guv side-footed the ball to Jamie, but he let it roll under his studs.

'Not you, too,' groaned Guv. 'What is it with everybody tonight?'

Ratso didn't know why Jamie had started playing like a slug on life support. He didn't really care. He had enough with his own problems, what with Gord giving him the cold shoulder, then Dad arriving at tea time. He'd turned up just as Mum was getting Dale out of the bath.

'Where is he?' Dad was shouting. 'Where's the big man that slaps an eleven-year-old boy about?'

If Dad was expecting some sort of apology, he was out of luck. Franny was out and Mum was in no mood for his outburst.

'I'm not having you come round here on the bounce,'

she yelled. She might be like putty in Franny's hands, but in Dad's she was pure gelignite. Ratso remembered what Jason had told him. Revenge? It sounded as good a reason as any for the way she was acting.

Dad got into even more of a lather. 'Don't you care if our Peter gets slapped around by some drunken layabout?'

To which Mum had an answer. 'Franny was stone cold sober and he isn't a layabout. He's out working at this very moment.'

Ratso tried to explain that he hadn't exactly got battered, but Dad wasn't listening. He wanted Franny's hide. Then or later, it didn't matter. Ratso looked at the helpless rage in his dad's face and he knew it wasn't just about the slap. It was about Mum and Dad and the split and everything. It was about them.

'You walked out on me, remember,' shrieked Mum. 'You and your stupid pride.'

In the end Mum cried and that started Dale off, too. Dad stormed out saying he'd be back and Mum yelled after him that he needn't bother. Ratso watched him drive off and felt sick to the pit of his stomach. He'd had a life, not much of one really, but a life nonetheless. Some bits were broken and others missing altogether. But it worked. Just about. So what did he do? He had to toss the whole thing up in the air and watch it smash to pieces on the floor.

Then Mum looked at him and asked if he was going to be late for footy. There was nothing he could do to set things straight, so he went.

'Look,' said Guv, breaking in on his thoughts, 'am I the only one doing this, or what?'

'Sorry, Guv,' Ratso murmured. 'Things on my mind. You know.'

Guv softened for a second, remembering his stupid mistake. 'Yes, I know.'

Practice had hardly resumed when Ronnie called everybody together. 'Right, lads, that'll do. I've got the team sheet if you want to know.'

'Shouldn't you leave it a couple of days?' asked Guv. 'Give us a chance to get in touch with Gord?'

Ratso shuffled his feet uneasily. It should have been him, not Guv, standing up for Gord. But what was the point? Gord didn't want to know.

'Sorry, Kev,' said Ronnie. 'I know you mean well, but I stick by the lads who stick by me. There's only one change for Sunday. Mattie ...'

Ratso saw the expectant grin on Mattie's face. He scowled and looked away.

'... You're in for Gordon.'

Six

Gord hadn't expected the taxi.

'Where's my dad?' he asked.

Mum opened the door of the black Hackney cab. 'Get in, Gordon, and I'll tell you.'

Gord did as he was told.

'How was the Youth Club?' asked Mum as the taxi pulled away.

'Fine.' It wasn't fine. It wasn't the Rough Diamonds. 'But where's my dad? How come you're picking me up in a cab?'

'He's gone to Manchester, that's why he's got the car.'

'Manchester, what for?'

'It's to do with work,' Mum explained. 'All the junior managers have been invited to a meeting.'

'But what's it for?' asked Gord. He could read his mum like a book, and Chapter One read Trouble.

'Your dad's had some bad news.'

'What?'

'Well,' said Mum. 'You know that promotion he was after?'

'Ye-es.' Gord knew all about it. It meant more money and more money meant that holiday to America. Disneyland included. 'Didn't he get it?'

'It's worse than that, I'm afraid. There have got to be cut-backs. The company is shutting one of its northern offices. It's either Manchester or Liverpool. One of them has got to close.'

'You mean we might have to move to Manchester?' Gord asked horrified. To a good Scouse lad it was the Evil Empire, the Land of the Mancs.

'No,' Mum replied slowly. 'I mean your dad could lose his job altogether.'

Gord's heart turned over. 'But we're going to Disneyland this year.'

'Not if they shut the office.'

'When will he know?' asked Gord. The Magic Kingdom was fading fast.

'Next couple of weeks,' Mum replied. 'Anyway, let's keep our fingers crossed.'

The cab pulled up in front of the house.

'Can I wait up for Dad?' asked Gord. OK, so he'd promised to hate the old man forever, but the news about his job had changed all that.

'It depends what time he gets in,' said Mum.

'If I help with the dishes? Please.'

Mum smiled. 'OK, if you help with the dishes you can have an extra half-hour.'

Why did I bother? thought Gord. Why did I rotten well bother?

He'd taken advantage of Dad's absence to use the PC. Doom 2 replaced the spread sheets. It was a daring thing to do. You usually had to plead like crazy to be allowed in Dad's precious study. Gord was just wasting a nest of alien guards with his pump shotgun when he heard the door go.

He met Dad in the hallway. 'Hi, Dad.'

His dad shook the rain off his overcoat. 'What are you doing up?'

Gord's heart took a nosedive. It hadn't been a good meeting. 'I was waiting for you.'

'Money, I suppose,' his dad snapped. 'What is it? Another school trip?'

'I don't want anything,' said Gord. 'I was waiting up for you, that's all.'

'What for?'

'Oh, Bobby,' said Mum, popping her head out of the living room. 'He wanted to see you.'

'So he's seen me,' said Dad. 'Now up to bed, Gordon. No son of mine stays up half the night.'

'It's only ten o'clock,' Gord complained.

'It's school tomorrow,' said Dad. 'Off you go.'

Gord looked at his mum, but she just held her hands out in a gesture of helplessness. Best leave well alone was the unspoken message. He hadn't even reached the top of his stairs when he heard the furious roar from his dad's study. 'Gordon!'

Gord turned. Uh-oh.

'Gordon!'

'I'm coming.'

Gord arrived outside the study door. 'What's up?' he asked nervously.

'This.' Dad was pointing at the computer screen.

'Its Doom,' said Gord.

'I know what it is,' said Dad. 'The point is: who gave you permission to play it?'

'I didn't think—'

'That's just the point, Gordon, you never do.'

'That's a bit unfair,' Mum protested.

But she was immediately overruled.

'What's more, you left it on. Do you want to damage the screen? Don't you know how to take care of anything?'

'I forgot.'

'Then there's this.'

Dad was warming to the task. Gord had a sneaking feeling he actually *enjoyed* losing his temper. He did it often enough! Dad was pointing to a sheaf of documents on the floor.

'Didn't you see all my papers, you great gorm?'

'Sorry.'

'If you've messed them up, you will be.'

Gord and Mum exchanged glances. The meeting must have gone really badly.

'Oh, get to bed,' said Dad. 'I'm going to put the figures from the meeting through the computer. I just know there's something they've overlooked.'

Gord fled from the room on the verge of tears. What was the point of even trying to be nice to him?

'Don't take it to heart,' whispered Mum, catching him at the top of the stairs. 'He's upset.'

'He's a pig!'

'Gordon!'

'Well, he is.'

'You can't call your father a pig,' Mum told him.

'Not even if he is one?'

'No. I mean yes. I mean ... Oh, you're being difficult. You're just like him sometimes.'

'I am not! If I was like him I'd cut my throat.'

'Gordon!'

'I would, with a rusty hacksaw. Honest I would.'

'Oh, what a dreadful thing to say.'

'I hate him,' Gord insisted. 'I hate him forever.'

'I think you'd better get to bed,' said Mum. 'You'll feel better in the morning.'

Gord shook his head. And Donald Duck would play in goal for Brazil!

Seven

'So where are this lot in the table?' Joey asked, indicating the departing St Patrick's team in their green and black stripes.

'I've already told you,' said Ratso tetchily.

'Then tell me again.'

'Fourth,' said Ratso, tying his laces. 'They're good, and all.'

'How good?' asked Daz.

Ratso took a deep breath, like he was sucking in the taste of all his misfortunes. Gord was still avoiding him, and Dad was on the warpath. He'd phoned every night asking for Franny, and every night Mum had hung up. But not until she'd given him a mouthful of abuse. Some of it should have had an 18 certificate.

Daz was waiting for his answer.

'You should pay attention to the games going on around you,' Ratso snapped. 'Goalies don't have much else to do.'

'So who's rubbed you up the wrong way?' asked Daz.

'He's still sore about Gord,' said Joey.

'Oh, don't tell me that's still going on,' groaned Daz.

In the corner of the changing rooms Mattie and Carl were smirking. It was still going on, and they were milking it for all they were worth.

'Serves you right,' said Mattie. 'This is what comes of ratting on your mates.'

'I didn't rat on anybody,' cried Ratso.

Only he had. Gord.

'You ratted on us,' said Carl. 'We had a deal and you copped out. Yes, Ratso the rat.'

'Oh, get stuffed.'

Carl reacted. So did Ratso. Suddenly they were toe to toe.

'Knock it off,' said Daz.

But Ratso and Carl carried on squaring up to one another.

'You heard what Daz said,' came a voice.

Guv was standing in the doorway. His appearance did the trick. Carl sat back on the slatted bench.

'So what's going on?' asked Guv.

'Nothing,' said Ratso.

'Yes, nothing,' said Carl.

Guv wasn't convinced. 'Mattie, have you got something to do with this?'

Mattie was staring down at his boots. 'Like they said, it was nothing.'

Guv glanced at Daz and Joey. 'You lot crack me up. You really do.'

'Anyway,' said Joey finally. 'I never did get an answer to my question. Tell me about St Pat's.'

'They beat Sefton Dynamoes last week,' said Ratso.

'How many?'

'Thirteen-one.'

'Thirteen!'

'Thirteen.'

'Crumbs.'

The rest of the team were arriving. There were a few rolled eyes at the news of St Pat's scoring exploits.

'Thirteen,' said Mattie, giving a low whistle. 'We'll have to defend well.'

The comment went down like a lead balloon.

'Let us down again,' snarled Ant, 'and you're dead.'

'Come on, lads,' said Ronnie, sticking his head round the changing room door. 'Let's be having you. This St Pat's lot are out already. They're dead keen.'

As the Diamonds clattered down the corridor in their boots, they heard laughter behind them.

'Well, if it isn't the One Point Wonders.'

It was Longmoor Celtic. They were really taking an interest in the Diamonds.

'We're not one-pointers any more,' Ratso shot back. 'We won last week.'

The Celtic lads started staggering about, as if they'd gone faint with the shock of it all.

'Stop messing,' said Guv. 'It's true. Seven-nil.'

'Yeah, but look who you were up against. Anybody can beat Warbreck.'

'Did you?'

'Only twelve-three, that's all.'

'Oh.'

'We've got you soon, haven't we?' said the Longmoor captain. 'The week after next.'

'We'll batter them, won't we, Nosmo?'

Ratso frowned. 'Why do you call him Nosmo?'

The Longmoor boys nudged the captain. 'His name's John King. It's like the signs in a café. No Smoking. Nosmo King. Get it?'

Ratso nodded. 'I wish I hadn't asked.'

'You're going to wish you hadn't played us,' said Nosmo. 'It's going to be more like a rugby score.'

'In your dreams,' said Ratso angrily. He'd been feeling brittle enough. This was all he needed.

'OK,' said Nosmo. 'We'll have you a bet. A fiver says we hammer you.'

'You're on,' said Ratso.

Satisfied with their morning's work, Longmoor jogged away.

'Oh, nice one, Ratso,' said Daz.

'What's up?'

'The bet, you divvy.'

'Well, they got to me.'

'I'll get to you if you do anything like that again,' said Ant.

'We'll look right meffs if we lose,' said John O'Hara.

'We won't lose,' said Ratso. 'We've got the blue and gold of Brazil on our backs. We're invincible.'

John started to say that their shirts were yellow not gold, but Ratso just ignored him. 'Now, let's get in the mood for the game. Listen to this.'

He snapped a cassette into the ghetto-blaster and the Diamonds took the field to the strains of *Ferry Across the Mersey*.

Within minutes of the kick-off it was more like Diamonds down the plughole. They were one-nil down, owing to a goalkeeping error. Daz had been back-pedalling to gather a cross when he fell backwards. Smack on his behind. His legs just went on strike. The ball bounced about for a second or two then one of the St Pat's attackers stabbed it in.

'What happened?' asked Jimmy Mintoe.

'Nothing,' said Daz, red-faced and angry with himself.

'Are you hurt?' asked Ant.

'I said,' Daz thundered, 'nothing happened, and I'm not hurt. I fell on my stupid bum, that's all.'

Which is about all that could be said on the matter. Enraged by the stupidity of the goal, the Diamonds threw everything at their opponents. Crosses from right and left, in-swingers, out-swingers, high balls, low crosses, long balls, short passes. Kitchen sink. Cuddly toy. They did everything. Except score.

And what happens when you press and press and don't turn the advantage into goals? That's right, you get hit on the break.

St Pat's got a free-kick five yards outside the penalty area. There didn't seem much danger, especially when they punted the ball aimlessly into the box. But Daz wasn't himself. He got another of his rushes of blood to the head. He charged out of his goal and flapped at the ball, finally presenting it at the feet of the same kid who'd given St Pat's the lead. He couldn't believe his luck, and rammed it home. Two-nil down.

'You berk!' roared Guv.

'Who are you calling a berk?' Daz yelled back.

'The great heap of dog's mess who gave away the second goal.'

It was only the timely arrival of Jamie and Dave that stopped them slugging it out right there in the goal-mouth. And that's the way it was at half-time. Two-nil down and two of the Diamonds' best players not even on speaking terms.

'Enjoying life at the bottom, are we?' asked Ronnie.

'What?'

'You like propping up the table?'

'Of course not.'

'Then start playing as a team.'

He said some other stuff, about tracking back and going on the overlap, but the main thing was playing as a team.

'Come on, lads,' said Guv. 'Let's get into them.'

They did too, with a vengeance, only to get hit on the break yet again. This time it was down to Mattie. He flung himself into a reckless tackle and left the right flank wide open. St Pat's were jubilant.

Three-nil up and not a single threat to their goal to speak of. Diamonds? Fool's gold, more like.

'Guv, Dave,' yelled Ronnie. 'Let Bash have the ball. We need some width.'

The change of tactics caught St Pat's napping. Bash was opening them up like a can opener. On his third run, Dave took the ball across the edge of the box before scuffing it into the net. Then Guv hit a screamer into the right-hand corner. Two-three down.

'That's it,' shouted Ronnie. 'Keep it down their end. Don't let them run with the ball. That's it. Tackle.'

Tackle was right. The Diamonds were flying in, especially Guv. He got a warning about going over the ball with his studs showing.

'It's a contact sport, isn't it?' he grumbled. 'What does this ref want, feather dusters at four hundred yards?'

With five minutes to go, Guv's tackling paid off. He dispossessed a nervy-looking winger in his own half and set off like a whippet. Exchanging a crisp one-two with Bashir, he powered into the box. The goal was an odd affair. As if nobody wanted to tackle him. They just let him run it into the net. The St Pat's manager went spare.

Less than a minute later, their goalie received a back pass. Instead of hitting it straight upfield, he looked for a pass to his defenders. That's when Guv did it. He roared like a wild animal. Then ran straight at the goalie. Like he was going to bolt down the lad's throat. The keeper lashed at the ball in panic and put it right into the path of Dave Lafferty. Dave side-footed it home and winked at Guv.

'Four-three up with a minute to go,' he said. 'We've got it in the bag.'

He'd counted without Mattie and Daz. From their last, desperate attack, St Pat's forced a corner. Daz hesitated. His confidence was shot.

Then he and Mattie went for it together, clashing heads and ending up in a tangled heap. Meanwhile the ball dropped gently into the back of the net.

That's how it ended, four apiece. It was a fair result, given the first-half performance. But Longmoor had won five-three on the next pitch and spent the next few minutes ribbing the Diamonds about their defence.

'Don't forget about our bet,' they called.

Ratso scowled. 'I haven't forgotten.'

'Bet you wish we had,' said Nosmo. 'Son, we're going to annihilate you.'

'Think so, do you?' shrieked Ratso. 'Well, I tell you what. Let's up the stakes. A tenner.'

'Why not make it fifteen?' asked Nosmo, delighted at Ratso's reaction.

'Done,' said Ratso. 'Fifteen it is.'

'Ratso,' hissed John O'Hara. 'Are you crazy?'

The blind fury was fading. Ratso looked around and realized what he'd done. He was crazy, all right.

Eight

Gord tossed the remote control on the couch. He was sick of channel surfing. Forty-three channels of utter rubbish.

'What's up, Gordon? Fed up?'

He nodded.

'You could always try another team,' his mum suggested.

But Gord didn't want another team. He wanted the Diamonds. It was driving him mad. Ratso had seemed so genuine. A real mate. Then in his mind's eye, Gord saw Carl and Mattie lurking in the corridor at school and he knew he'd been had.

'No, I've had it with footy,' said Gord. He wanted it to sound final, but it still tore his guts out to say it.

'We'll find you something else,' said Mum. It was meant to cheer him up.

Wonderful, thought Gord. That's her answer to everything. A nice little hobby for our Gord. But he didn't want a nice little hobby. He didn't want pond dipping, or face painting or Rearing Stick Insects for Beginners. He wanted some mates.

'Anyway,' said Mum, 'we're going to your nan's. That'll be nice.'

'Scintillating,' snorted Gord.

Mum gave him a funny look, but she didn't say anything.

'Where's Dad?' asked Gord.

'Out, thank goodness,' Mum replied.

'Where's he gone?'

'Just out.' She paused. 'I showed him the door. He was getting on my nerves. Brooding about work. I mean, thinking about it all the time won't make things any better.'

Gord followed her into the kitchen. Mum started peeling potatoes.

'Doesn't he know anything yet?' asked Gord.

'No.'

Mum was peeling for all she was worth. As if she had Dad's face under the knife.

'Mum …'

'Yes, love?'

'You'll have no potato left.'

She looked down at the sliver of potato. 'Oh.' She smiled, then laughed. 'Oops.'

'Here,' said Gord. 'I'll give you a hand. You're not happy, are you?'

'I'll swing for him,' said Mum. 'Honest to God, I'll end up throwing something at him. Like your nan. I'll never forget. When I was about eight, your grandad came home drunk at dinner time. She threw the teapot at him.'

'Never!'

'She did. Wouldn't think she had it in her, would you?'

Gord shook his head. 'So what's Dad done?'

'Got a few hours to spare?' she asked.

'No, but I'll take the shortened version,' Gord said with a laugh in his voice.

'You know your dad,' she started. 'With his big ideas.'

'Ye-es.'

'Well, he's done something stupid.'

'Ye-es.'

'He wasn't just hoping for that promotion,' Mum explained. 'He thought he'd got it in the bag. He's already spent the money in advance.'

'How do you mean?'

'The holiday in the States, a new conservatory, some other bits and bobs. He's already put down big deposits. If he does lose his job we'll be left owing thousands.'

'Oh.'

'He's really worried. I do understand how he feels ...'

But. There just had to be a but.

'But he's driving me up the wall!'

Gord smiled. There was the *But*, right on cue.

'You know what he was up to at seven o'clock this morning?'

'No.'

'He only had the last three years' sales figures spread out on the floor. He kept going on and on at me, showing me one column of figures after another. He's obsessed.'

'I know,' said Gord sympathetically.

'He really knows how to get under my skin.'

Tell me about it, thought Gord. Didn't she know how many years grief he'd had off Dad?

'I suppose what I'm saying is this: we'll have to keep our heads down until all this is sorted out. And that means no winding him up.'

Gord's mouth dropped open. *Me* wind *him* up!

'Just humour him. He was made up when you gave up the football team.' She smiled. 'Come to think of it, I was relieved myself. Those boys were a bit wild.'

Gord frowned. They weren't wild. They were alive, that's all. Not mummified at home. He thought about Ratso following him around at school, making his stupid excuses. Maybe he should have listened … No, what was the point? Ratso had betrayed him.

'So you will make an effort, won't you, Gordon? Humour him, just for me. Life will be purgatory otherwise.'

Gord nodded.

'Good,' said Mum. 'Oh, talk of the devil, here he is now.'

Gord watched the car pull into the driveway.

'Do you think he's in a good mood?' asked Mum hopefully.

Dad slammed the car door and stamped into the house. His eyebrows were knotted in a V-shaped tangle. Gord pulled a face and Mum laughed. It was the last laughter heard in the house for a couple of hours.

'Is Gordon in?' asked Ratso.

Gord peered round his dad's back. Ratso was standing on the doorstep, still in his football kit.

'He is, but you're not seeing him.'

'But it was all a mistake, Mr Jones. Honest, I just want to explain.'

Gord wasn't sure what to make of it. The way Ratso had been creeping round him at school, that was one thing. But plucking up the courage to face the wrath of Nosun, that was something else. It made Gord think.

'The mistake, Peter Ratcliffe, was doing the dirty on our Gordon in the first place.'

'But that's what I want to explain,' said Ratso. 'I wasn't going along with Mattie and Carl at all. That's what I've been trying to tell him. When Guv warned him, he'd been jumping to conclusions. You know Guv.'

'Do you think I'm completely puddled?' demanded Gord's dad. 'Now clear off.'

'Can't I just talk to him for a minute?' Ratso pleaded.

'N-O spells no,' said Dad.

And P-I-G spells Dad, thought Gord. He was desperate to hear what Ratso had to say. He'd made the lad suffer, but he was suffering too.

'Dad,' he whispered, tugging at his shirt-sleeve.

'Get back in the house,' said Dad. 'Peter is just leaving.'

'No I'm not,' retorted Ratso, emboldened by Gord's appearance in the doorway. 'Listen, Gord. You've got it all wrong. Ask Guv—'

'McGovern!' Dad bellowed. 'Do you think we're going to believe anything *he* tells us? Now clear off before I run you off.'

Dad closed the door.

'But that's not fair,' said Gord. 'It's me he wanted to talk to.'

'Have you forgotten what happened?' demanded Dad. 'It's only last Sunday you were crying your eyes out. They were picking on you, remember. Three on to one. Or doesn't that matter any more?'

'He did say it was a mix-up.'

Dad rolled his eyes. 'And you're stupid enough to believe him? Grow up, Gordon. You're finished with those young hooligans and that's that. Now get ready to go to your nan's.'

'But Dad …'

'Up those stairs. *Now.*'

Gord knew defeat when it stared him in the face. He hadn't stood up to his dad in eleven years, and he didn't have the courage to start now.

From his bedroom window Gord watched Ratso trailing away. He found himself feeling almost sorry for him. He was still at the window when Dad yelled up the stairs.

'Have you got changed yet? We're leaving in ten minutes and you're not going in a pair of dirty old jogging pants.'

Suddenly Gord was sorry for himself.

Nine

It wasn't a good day for me either, that Sunday. First, we threw away two points, then I waited all afternoon for my dad. He'd promised to take me out. But he didn't show. I flew to the window every time a car pulled up, but it was no use. He'd let me down … yet again. I got to thinking.

Bobby Jones is an idiot, but at least he's there for Gord. And OK, so Ratso's mum and dad have split up, but he still sees them, both of them. What a turn up for the book, eh? I started off trying to make something of these two pathetic specimens, soft lad and the clown. All of a sudden, I'm jealous of them. Anyway, back to the old man. About five o'clock, Mum calls me in from the garden where I'm playing kicky-up.

'It's your dad,' she says, disapproving as usual.

He was phoning from his mobile. A dead give-away, that. It meant he was out on business with Lee Ramage. Business! That was a good word for it. Drugs, I'll bet, or stolen gear. He's going to end up inside one of these days.

'Sorry,' he says. 'But I got held up. Maybe next week-end.'

And that was it. He hung up.

Next weekend. Oh yeah, I believe that. With my old man, next weekend never comes. Still, I'm not the sort to lie down and die. I still had the Diamonds. Sometimes I think they're all I've got. Well, there's no point mooning around waiting for my old man to start acting like a father, is there? Sure, I've still got Mum and Gareth, but the Diamonds are my real family. Home's just a place I doss down half the time. It's only when I'm in the blue and gold that I feel alive. On the pitch I'm not just some sad kid who's been dumped by his dad, I'm a hero. But a hero needs backup, and the Diamonds had a way to go to come up with the goods.

If the game against St Pat's had told me anything, it was that we needed Gord. What he lacked in aggression he made up in sheer, natural strength. Unfortunately, there was only one person who could get him back, and that was Ratso. I thought, maybe he needed a hand. Then I remembered what a mess I'd made of things the first time round. Now I knew what it must feel like to be a manager. You know what needs to be done, but you can't get out there on the field of play and sort it.

I just had to hope Ratso had the nous to do something about it by himself.

Ten

'OK', said Gord. 'Now you've got my undivided attention. So what have you got to say to me?'

It was a different Gord speaking. He'd always been a soft touch. He knew he had. Desperate for somebody to call a friend, hanging round the others like a faithful old dog. Now he was getting something his parents' protectiveness had denied him, the scar tissue on your heart that stops you getting hurt too easily.

Ratso leant back against the playground wall. They were in the breeze-block alcove where the wheelie bins were stored. It was about the closest you came to privacy in the school yard at Our Lady's. He was going to have to play a blinder. Sure, he wanted Gord back as a mate. But he couldn't forget the little fact of the bet with Longmoor. Without Gord in defence they didn't stand a chance. And where was he going to get fifteen quid if they lost? He'd given three weeks pocket money to Jason for Dale's birthday present.

'I'd never have gone through with it,' he said.

'No?' Gord wasn't going to give Ratso an inch. He was going to have to prove himself.

'No. It was all Mattie's idea.'

'So you're trying to tell me you didn't set me up?'

'No … I mean … Well, I *was* going along with it.' Ratso didn't like the way that sounded. 'Sort of.'

Gord's eyes narrowed. 'Either you were or you weren't.'.

'They were my mates,' said Ratso feebly. This wasn't going the way he'd planned it.

Gord shook his head impatiently. 'I thought I was, too.'

'You were ... are.'

'Oh yeah? It sounds like it, doesn't it?' Gord made as if to walk away.

'Hang on.'

Gord was almost enjoying himself. He was feeling something new, power over somebody else. Ratso was going to have to work his way back into his good book – even if he did believe his story.

'Dad was right,' said Gord. 'This is a load of rubbish.'

'No,' said Ratso brightly. He felt a joke coming on. 'That's rubbish.' He pointed at the wheelie bins.

'Ratso,' Gord told him. 'Your sense of humour is as lame as your excuses.'

Idiot, thought Ratso. Why did I have to play the fool? 'You've got to listen to me, Gord lad.'

'Have I? Then tell me something worth hearing.'

'I told Mattie and Carl where to get off. I was taking a risk, you know. They'd have done me over but for Guv.'

'Yes?'

'Yes. I never did anything, you see. I just didn't stand up to them. You must think I'm a spineless little get –'

'Took the words right out of my mouth,' said Gord, interrupting.

Ratso smiled ruefully. 'OK, I asked for that one. It's true, though. They wanted me to set you up, but I kept putting them off. The day of the Warbreck game, they were getting fed up of waiting. They were on my back about it all the time. That's when I told them to get another mug.'

'That right?' Gord still looked sceptical, and it wasn't all an act to make Ratso grovel.

'What have I got to do, Gord? I'm telling the truth.'

He was about to continue when he saw Dale approaching, holding his teacher's hand.

'Ah, there you are, Peter,' said Mrs Atherton. 'I'm afraid Dale's rather upset this morning. Do you think you could have a word with him?'

Ratso knew what was bothering his little brother. His seventh birthday and there had been no present from Dad that morning. No card either. Not even a phone call. It had been a battle to get him to school at all.

Gord edged away.

'Hang on, Gord.'

Mrs Atherton glanced at Gord, then back at Ratso. 'I think Dale comes first,' she said. 'Don't you?'

Ratso watched Gord walk away.

'All right, Miss, I'll do my best.'

Come home-time, Ratso was hanging round the school gates. Mum and Franny were taking him, Aaron and Dale to the Snow Zone straight from school so he had to wait with them. It was Dale's birthday treat. Ratso had had a frustrating day all round. He'd hoped to catch Gord at dinner time, but it had been wet breaks all day. What's more, he'd been called twice to Dale's classroom. He'd been crying in class and the school couldn't get Mum on the phone. Ratso felt sorry for Dale, but impatient, too. Right now, he was more bothered about Gord. He caught sight of Dale and Aaron coming out of school, but it wasn't good news. Mrs Atherton had Dale by the hand. He'd been crying again.

'Leave him with me, Miss.'

'Dale tells me your mum's picking you up,' said Mrs Atherton.

'That's right,' said Ratso, craning round as he searched for Gord.

'Do you think she could pop in and see the Head. Mrs Hale's concerned about Dale.'

'I'll tell her,' said Ratso. Mum was going to love that. Getting called in to school. 'Oh, give over, Dale,' he said as Mrs Atherton walked back into the classroom. 'You'll wear your face out.'

'Not going to be much fun at the Snow Zone, is it?' asked Aaron.

'Not if he carries on snivelling,' said Ratso. He was still looking for Gord.

That's when he heard Mum's voice. She was waving from up the road. 'Get a move on, lads. I want to beat the traffic.'

'We can't go yet,' said Ratso. 'Mrs Hale wants to see you.'

'Mrs Hale? Why?' Then she noticed Dale's face. She knelt down and dabbed at Dale's eyes with a flowered hankie.

'What's up, love?' she asked. 'Still upset about your dad?'

That did it. Dale started sobbing again.

Great, thought Ratso. Fat chance I've got of sorting things with Gord. Then it got worse still. Who should arrive at the gallop but Dad. He was red-faced and panting, and he was carrying Dale's present. 'Thank goodness,' he said. 'I was afraid I'd miss you, son. Sorry I'm late with the pressie. I got called into work unexpectedly. I'd never forget your birthday. Still, all's well that ends well.'

Except it didn't end well. Dale and Aaron shot off to

a corner of the playground to unwrap the present, so they missed most of the fun. Ratso didn't. He had to watch the whole thing. Dad was about to follow the boys to watch Dale's face as he opened the package when he saw Franny sitting in the car.

'Now don't start,' warned Mum, alert to the danger.

She could have saved her breath. Dad went ape. Talk about the red mist falling. He just blew his cool completely.

'Excuse me,' he said between thin, curled lips. 'I'd like a word with you.'

Dad put a hand on the car roof and stared down at Franny.

'Please, Sean,' said Mum. 'Not here.'

'I just want to know something,' said Dad, wrenching the door open. 'I want to know why a grown man slaps somebody else's son about.'

Franny was trying to close the door.

'All you have to do,' said Dad, 'Is apologize to Peter and I'll forget the whole thing.'

Only the way he said it, Ratso didn't believe him. Franny was the wall between Mum and Dad, and he was about to get knocked down.

'Apologize?' said Franny. 'To a snotty-nosed kid. You a comedian?'

'No,' said Dad. 'I'm dead serious.'

Mum was tugging at his sleeve. Some of the parents collecting their children were starting to take an interest. So was Mrs Hale. Ratso could see her watching from her office window.

'Get lost,' said Franny.

But Dad didn't get lost. He leant forward and dragged Franny out of the car. That's when Franny did it. He threw a punch. Dad did the same. Then they tussled for a moment, before falling over the wall into a garden. For a moment everybody stared at them, two grown men wrestling among some gnomes. After that it was bedlam. Everybody was screaming and shouting. A few of the parents were trying to separate them, and the householder had appeared on his lawn yelling about his gnomes.

'You're going to break them,' he shouted. 'And I've only just replaced them.'

'Sean, Franny!' Mum was crying. 'Oh, stop them somebody.'

It was easier said than done.

'First kids nicking them,' said the gnome-owner. 'Now this!'

'Oh, shut up about your rotten gnomes,' said Mum.

That only made things worse. Suddenly, not only were Dad and Franny fighting on the ground, but this old bloke was following Mum around demanding that she apologize to him.

It was Mrs Hale who finally sorted things out. She marched out of school, clapped her hands, and told them to stop. In her best morning assembly voice. And they did. Like guilty schoolkids.

'Look,' wailed the gnome-owner. 'You've broken his fishing rod.'

'Clear off before I break *your* fishing rod,' seethed Mum.

He was speechless, which was a relief.

'Do you know something?' Mum said right into Dad's face. 'I won't ever talk to you again. Ever!'

Dad's shoulders sagged, 'But She, you've got to listen to me. It's important.'

Mum dismissed him with a toss of the head.

Dale was standing next to Aaron. He was clutching his new space cruiser and staring at his mud-spattered father. 'Why's Dad dirty?' he asked.

'I'm sorry,' said Dad, defeat showing in his face. 'So sorry.'

That's when Ratso finally saw Gord. He was standing with his dad, watching the fracas. He looked dismayed. Bobby Jones looked delighted.

Ratso heard what he said to Gord. 'That really the sort of mate you want, Gordon? Over my dead body.'

Eleven

Ratso hadn't said a word all morning. There had been plenty of opportunity. His class and Gord's had been waiting outside the hall as the infants filed in for assembly. But not a word. Ratso had just stared at the floor. It was the same at dinner-time. Ratso had just followed the netball line round the yard. Like a train on a track. He was completely zombified. By half past twelve Gord had had enough. His curiosity got the better of him. He followed the netball line from the other end of the yard and came face to face with Ratso. Or rather face to lowered forehead.

'What's up, Ratso?'

'You were there,' said Ratso dully. 'You saw what happened.'

'The fight, you mean?'

'What else? Everybody's been skitting me over it.'

'They'll soon forget about it,' said Gord.

'You reckon? You should hear Mattie and Carl. They're loving it.'

Gord smiled. 'Yes, I'll bet. I believe you about the set-up, you know.'

'Really?'

'Of course. I knew you were telling the truth when you showed up at our house.'

'Then how come you never let on?'

'Dunno,' said Gord. 'It doesn't make much difference, though.'

Ratso raised his eyes from the netball line. 'How come?'

'What do you think? Dad laid down the law about the Diamonds. He won't let me play for them again.'

'Tight beggar,' said Ratso. He could wave the fifteen quid goodbye. 'We could do with you this Sunday.'

'Who is it, Longmoor?'

'No,' Ratso replied. 'That's a week on Sunday. It's Ajax. Top of the league.'

'I'd love to play in that one,' said Gord wistfully. 'I hate my dad.'

'Join the club. I hate mine, too. I can't believe he went for Franny. Not on Dale's birthday. Mum says she won't let him see us again.'

'Can she do that?'

'I don't think so,' said Ratso, 'But it's like living in a war zone.'

'Same at ours,' said Gord. 'Dad thinks he's going to get made redundant. It's made him twice as bad as usual.'

'Is that possible?' asked Ratso.

'Unfortunately it is.'

They wandered over to the railings and stared out at the waste ground opposite. From their vantage point they could see Mersey Park on the hill and the maisonettes on the fringe of the Diamond with their flaking paint and graffiti.

'I'm not looking forward to the Longmoor game,'

said Ratso.

'I thought you said it was Ajax this week.'

'It is.'

'Then what's so important about Longmoor?'

Ratso took a deep breath. 'You couldn't lend me fifteen quid, could you?'

'Fifteen quid! What do you think I am, Barclays Bank?'

'Compared to me you are,' Ratso replied. 'We're always skint. I thought you'd be minted. You know, a nice little savings account.'

'Oh, I've got one of them, but Dad's got the book. He says it's for when I go to university.'

'University! But that's years off.'

'One of his big ideas,' said Gord. 'It's a wonder he hasn't already got me booked in. Anyway, why do you need fifteen quid?'

'For the bet.'

'What bet?'

'Nobody's told you, then?'

Ratso turned and rested his back against the railings. 'Do you know Nosmo?'

Gord shook his head.

'The Longmoor captain. He tricked me into it. I bet him fifteen quid we'd beat them. Not too clever, was it?'

'That, Ratso lad, is an understatement. Where are you going to get the money from?'

'I could win the Lottery,' said Ratso, 'or else I'll get battered. And when Longmoor have done with me, the Diamonds will finish the rest.'

'So you could do with a miracle?'

'Got any?'

'No.'

'Then I'm dead.'

Twelve

Gord had been building himself up to it ever since his talk with Ratso. Three times he'd put it off, but now it was do or die. It was eight o'clock on Sunday morning. Who knows, if he could win Dad over, Ronnie might even put him on the sub's bench.

'Are we doing anything today?' asked Gord.

Dad peered over the *Observer*. 'I beg your pardon?'

'Have you got anything planned?'

'We're going to your nan's this afternoon, if that's what you mean. You can help me do her garden. Her arthritis has been playing her up again.'

'Dad ...' Gord could see his mum watching anxiously. She'd twigged what he was after.

Down came the *Observer* for the second time. 'Yes, Gordon?'

'Seeing we're not doing anything till after dinner ...' His voice trailed off.

'Yes?'

'Could I go and watch the Diamonds?' Easy does it, he told himself. One step at a time. 'Just watch, I mean.'

Dad shook the *Observer* irritably. 'No chance.'

'But I'd only be watching. Ronnie wouldn't put me in the team. I mean, I missed Monday training and you know what he's like over that.'

He knew he was rushing his words.

'Now stop right there, Gordon Jones,' said Dad. He always used Gord's full name when he was annoyed. 'If I've told you once, I've told you a dozen times. You've finished with them. Fertig, finito, finis. Got it?'

Dad gave a strangled growl and stamped into the study to read his paper.

'I told you it wasn't worth it,' said Mum. 'He's worried sick over his job.'

'That's no reason to take it out on me,' said Gord.

'No, of course not, but ...'

'It isn't my fault, is it?'

'No.'

'So why won't he let me do anything?'

That's when he saw Mum's expression change. He knew the scene. He'd watched it in a dozen horror films. The bit when the hero realizes the monster's just walked up behind him. Gord felt a hot flush down his back.

'Finished shouting the house down?' asked Dad icily.

Gord turned slowly.

'Let's have it, then,' Dad demanded. 'You've been keen enough to take a pop at me behind my back. Let's have it, lad. If you've got something to say, just spit it out.'

Gord could feel a lump rising in his throat. 'I want to start playing for the Diamonds again. Ratso explained everything.'

'What, like his father brawling with his mother's ... toy boy?'

Gord almost burst out laughing. A toy boy Franny wasn't!

'And what are you smirking at?'

Gord knew the smile had been a bad idea. 'I wasn't ...'

Dad turned to Mum for support. 'See what happens when he hangs round with the likes of McGovern and Ratcliffe. He starts cheeking his parents.'

'I wasn't!'

'See, you're at it again.'

'You're being stupid,' cried Gord. Dad had driven him past the point of no return.

'Go to your room!'

'I won't!'

Dad took him by the arm and started marching him towards the stairs. Gord was wriggling and writhing.

'Get off me. Gerroff!'

He lashed out with his foot and caught his dad on the calf. Dad recoiled, stunned by Gord's reaction. Then his eyes narrowed.

'Bobby,' said Mum, stepping between them. 'Don't.'

But he just barged past her. His face was red and blotchy and the skin was drawn tight over his cheek-bones.

'Get up those stairs. Now!'

'Drop dead,' yelled Gord.

'Don't you start screaming at me, lad,' roared Dad. 'Raise your voice at me and I'll …'

Gord flinched, expecting a backhander. Instead, there was a strange groan.

'Unnnhhhh!'

'Bobby,' said Mum. 'Bobby, what's wrong?'

'My chest,' gasped Dad. 'Phone an ambulance. Quick, I think I'm having a heart attack.'

Then everything was happening in freeze frames. Like in a dream. Mum was reaching for the phone and dialling. At the same time Dad was sinking to his knees, holding his chest. Gord watched in horror as he knelt on the carpet, gasping for breath.

'Mum,' murmured Gord as she replaced the receiver. 'I've killed my dad.'

Thirteen

'So what's this?' Guv demanded. 'Have we turned into a registered charity, or what?'

'Sorry, Guv,' said Mattie.

'You will be. The next time you get the ball on the edge of the box,' Guv told him, 'just clear it. Nothing fancy. Don't even think about finding your own men. Kick it out of play. Get rid upfield. Anything. Just don't hand it to them on a plate.'

Ratso looked at the ball nestling forlornly in the back of the net, and Daz flinging his gloves after it. The Diamonds were four-two down, and after holding a two-one lead early in the match. It's not like they weren't playing good stuff. Dave, Bash and Guv could go through the Ajax defence at will. The trouble is, Ajax were taking the Diamonds apart at the back even quicker. They were missing Gord like crazy.

'Now, come on!' roared Guv. He wasn't captain for nothing.

'A win today,' Ratso offered helpfully, 'and we could finally be off the bottom. Red House Rovers are only two points above us.'

'There you go,' said Guv. 'You heard what Ratso said. So what do you intend doing about it? Are you planning to stay losers forever?'

Jamie tapped the ball to Dave to restart. Dave glanced up and lofted it out to Bash. But he'd made a few too many good runs down the left. Ajax had wised up to the threat and they'd put two on him. Bashir jinked and teased but there was no way through. Turning, he rolled the ball back to Ratso.

'Ratso,' Dave was shouting. 'In the air, Rats.'

But Jimmy Mintoe had made a run far side and looked a better bet. Ratso struck it with all his strength. To his relief it reached Jimmy. Taking it to the goal line, he hit it hard and low. Dave threw himself at it and saw it bounce in off his chest.

The Diamonds were only three-four down and in with a shout.

'Now,' Guv ordered. 'This time let's keep it tight.'

He may as well have saved his breath. From the re-start, Ajax put it down the middle of the field. And tried to meet the dropping ball on the volley, only to miss it completely. Suddenly it was two Ajax attackers on to one defender. And that defender just had to be Mattie.

'Clear it!' shouted Guv.

Mattie's first touch looked good. He brought it down with his chest. But that's when he blew it. Seeing Jimmy racing back he tried to put it out to his left.

'Who does he think he is?' groaned Guv. 'Jamie flipping Redknapp?'

Mattie had put it smack into the path of an Ajax player. Unable to believe his luck, the lad ran on strongly and slotted it past Daz. Three-five.

'What was that?' stormed Guv. 'After everything I've said to you.'

'Sorry, Guv,' said Mattie.

'You will be,' said Guv. 'You will be. If in doubt, launch it. No more pratting about. You don't have the skill.'

After half-time Guv pulled one back with a low shot that bounced and bobbled in the rutted area before beating the Ajax goalie, only to see Joey Bannen put through his own goal less than a minute later. Four-six. With a couple of minutes to go, Mattie gifted Ajax a free kick. They could only manage a soft shot but it hit Ant's shoulder and deflected against the crossbar. It was a formality for the Ajax striker to put it away.

'Come back, Gord,' said Jamie. 'All is forgiven.'

'Amen,' said John O'Hara.

'Don't be too hard on Mattie,' said Ronnie at the final whistle. 'He did his best.'

'Then I'd hate to see his worst,' said Guv. He flung his shin-guards at Mattie. 'Moron!'

'Now that's enough, Kevin,' warned Ronnie. 'We're a team and we don't start yelling and screaming at each other.'

'He could do with a bit of shouting and screaming,' said Guv, glaring venomously at Mattie. 'In fact, he could do with a cattle prod. It might wake him up.'

Guv was a great captain as long as you were doing the business. But let the side down and he was at you like an atomic polecat. Especially when he knew you'd done something rotten to one of the other players.

'Enough!' said Ronnie. 'Go and cool off. I'll see you all on Monday night.'

That was the clue for the Longmoor boys, of course. They were just coming away from their own game on Pitch Five.

'Get a bit of a roasting, did you, lads?' asked Nosmo.

'Seven-four,' said Ant. 'What about you?'

'Six-three,' he answered. 'Only we won. Something tells me we're going to wallop you next week. Want to up the bet to twenty?'

John O'Hara glared at Ratso. 'You keep your mouth shut.'

'Will you listen to that?' said Nosmo. 'Even they know they can't beat us.'

'Get lost,' said Ratso. 'We'll murder you.'

'I hope you've got the money,' said John, as Longmoor strolled away. 'Because nobody else is going to be bailing you out, big mouth.'

Ratso managed a smile. 'No problem.'

But it was.

It was the third time Ratso had sneaked upstairs in the space of half an hour.

'Something wrong with your bladder, Peter?' called Mum. 'Nobody needs the toilet that often.'

There was nothing wrong with his bladder, just his life. Defeat at the hands of Ajax, then Mum and Franny cuddling in the living room as he came in from the game. It was the final straw. It was bad enough her barring his dad from the house, but messing about with that retard right in front of him – there couldn't have been a worse insult.

'What are you up to, squirt? asked Jason, poking his head out of his bedroom.

'Nothing. Keeping out of their way. Franny's got his hands all over Mum again.'

'I know. Makes you sick, doesn't it? Anyway, I'm off out with Tracey. See you later.'

'Yes, see you, Jase.'

Ratso listened for the back door. Good, Jase had gone.

'What are you doing, Pete?' asked Dale from the hallway.

'Minding my own business,' Ratso retorted. 'Ever tried it?'

Dale stamped away, grumbling. Ratso took a deep breath. Couldn't he get a minute's peace round this place? He listened for a couple of minutes, then edged into Mum's bedroom. As he thought of Mum and Franny, he suddenly thought nothing of taking the money. There was the purse on Mum's bedside table. She'd collected child benefit on Thursday, so it would be bulging with notes. There was no hesitation, just anger at Mum and the need for the money. Slowly, Ratso eased open the clip and peeled off three fivers.

'Peter,' called Mum, 'What are you doing up there?'

Heart thumping, he flew to the door. 'I'm looking for my trainers. Have you seen them?'

'Seen them,' she chuckled, 'I can smell them from here. They're in the magazine rack.'

'Oh, ta.'

He flew down the stairs, pulled on his trainers and shot out of the house. All in the time it took to say Stop Thief!

It was only when he was turning the corner into South Parade that it hit him, a wave of heat that swept through him from his head to his stomach. He knew now, guilt wasn't just a word. It was a virus that filled you with pain and sickness. And he'd got it.

PART THREE

Blood Pressure

One

Sunday was the pits. We were on the floor, every one of us. Ronnie tried to lift us, but we weren't having any. After the cup win over Blessed Hearts we thought we'd turned the corner, we really did. Now here we were, still rooted to the bottom of the table. It was a nightmare. I'd given my all rebuilding this team, and suddenly we were back to square one. I was stumped. I mean, Dave and I were knocking in the goals and Bashir was the speed king out on the flanks. It was our defence. It had no backbone. I can hardly believe I'm saying this, but Gord was the rock we needed to build on. That's right, I do mean soft lad. With every game it became more obvious that he was the missing ingredient.

And what a let-down Ratso had turned out to be. I'd been relying on him to get Gord back, but he was as much use as a rubber magnet. I could hardly get a word out of him. He just trailed around with his chin on the floor, making everybody depressed. He looked like he'd got the burdens of the world on his shoulders. I'd have to do something after all.

Two

Gord felt like his guts had been kicked out. What sort of a kid gives his dad a heart attack? He looked around the blank walls of Fazakerley Hospital. He'd only been in a hospital once before. That was the time he fell and knocked out three front teeth on his nan's coffee table. What's up with me, he thought suddenly. There's my dad on his death bed and I'm thinking about teeth! He had to be the worst kid in the universe, the absolute pits.

His mum had gone in to see the doctor. What was going to happen to him? What did they do to dad-killers anyway? Gord saw nurses and doctors hurrying along the corridor, and wondered if they knew. He was there, sitting in their hospital, Gordon Dad-Killer Jones. It was all too much for him. There he was, sitting on the bench seat, thinking that everybody knew what he'd done. Maybe they were pretending not to know about him, just so he wouldn't leg it before the coppers came for him. Then his mind really started to race. What if they took him away? What if they locked him up? John O'Hara reckoned Guv nearly got put away. He used to set fires. John said you got banged away whether you were a kid or not. Gord shivered. They might stick him in with any old nutter. He was scared witless. He could just see himself in a cell at Walton prison.

'What's your name?' he'd ask his cell mate.

'Kermit the Frog,' he'd answer, hopping off the top bunk. 'What's yours. Ribbit, ribbit.'

Then Mum returned. Gord shot to his feet in a panic. He didn't want to be stuck away with Kermit the Frog. Or any other sort of super-charged pyscho, for that matter.

Only he didn't say that. Just: 'Is he … ?'

'No, your dad isn't going to croak, love.'

Gord nearly swallowed his tongue. Was Mum telepathic or something? How did she know about Kermit the Frog?

Mum sat down and patted the seat. 'Come and sit down. You'll see your dad in a minute.'

'You mean we're going on to the ward?'

In his mind's eye he saw his dad looking up accusingly from his bed of pain, a posse of detectives firing questions and a stenographer taking down his confession.

'What ward? He's coming home with us.'

'Home!'

Mum smiled. 'That's right.'

'But what about his heart?'

'It wasn't his heart at all.'

Not his heart! Gord's mind started racing. Not cancer. Not the Big C. 'You mean he's got ...'

Mum read his mind. 'No, not that either.' She paused. 'It was indigestion.'

Indigestion, thought Gord. He'd been torturing himself on account of a stray Sugar Puff? So what was it, cardiac arrest or a half-chewed Kit Kat?

'You what?'

'Indigestion,' Mum repeated. 'And stress.'

Stress. Gord had heard about stress. It was like pressure. And Dad had given him enough of that in his time.

'I don't get it,' said Gord. 'He was lying on the carpet. He couldn't even breathe.'

'I know,' said Mum. 'It looked bad, didn't it? But the doctor says he's fine. Heart like a lion. Blood pressure's a bit on the high side, though.'

That word again. Pressure.

'But there's nothing wrong with your dad that a bit more relaxation and a bit less worry wouldn't put right.'

Suddenly Gord stopped being scared. He was relieved. And angry. Indigestion! Stress! For crying out loud. He'd thought the old man was going to snuff it.

'Talk of the devil,' said Mum. 'Here he is now.'

And there he was, large as life and twice as ugly. And not a tube or drip or wire hooked up to a bleeping machine. Gord was disappointed.

'So you didn't crash?' he asked.

'Crash? I wasn't even in a car.'

Mum shook her head. 'He means a heart attack.'

Dad looked around sheepishly, as if he didn't want anybody to know he'd been in hospital with indigestion. 'Let's go home,' he said. He sounded very subdued.

'Suits me,' said Mum. 'I've had enough excitement for one Sunday.'

They were halfway down the corridor when Gord stopped.

'Dad.'

'Yes, son?'

'I'm sorry.'

Dad gave a thin smile.

'Yes, me too.'

Three

'How did it go yesterday?' asked Gord.

'Awful. Ajax slammed us seven-three.'

Gord glanced across the school yard at Mattie. 'So how did he do?'

'Played like a duck-billed platypus with a broken leg,' said Ratso. 'Chronic. You've got to get back in the side, Gord. For my sake. Then I could give this back.' He produced the three fivers.

'Where did you get that?' asked Gord.

'Nicked it. Out of Mum's purse.'

'You never!'

'I did. I don't know what got into me. She just made me mad. Her and that Franny.'

Gord was appalled. 'But you can't go taking money. What if you get caught? If that was my parents, I'd be grounded for life.' He pictured his dad. 'Or even longer.'

Ratso shrugged his shoulders. 'I didn't think.'

Gord stared at the money.

'Mum already knows it's gone,' said Ratso. 'She was quizzing our Jase about it this morning. She wanted to know how he could afford to take Tracey to the pictures. I sneaked out to school before she could ask me but I'll be next.'

'What are you going to do with it?' asked Gord.

'Hide it, I suppose.'

'Where?'

Ratso thought for a moment, then looked hopefully at Gord.

'Oh no,' said Gord. 'If you think I'm going to …'

'But you're my mate.'

'Dad would kill me.'

'Please. It's only for a few days. Until the match.'

'I can't.'

'Well, I can't keep it,' said Ratso. 'Mum's bound to go through my trouser pockets.'

Gord gave a long, shuddering sigh. 'OK, hand it over.' He took the money and stuffed it into his back pocket. 'But don't ever ask me to do anything like this again.'

'You're a mate, Gord.'

'I'm a mug.'

Ratso winked. 'I owe you one.'

Gord shook his head. 'I reckon you owe me at least two.'

Ratso remembered the set-up. 'Oh yes, I forgot.'

'If Dad found this money, it'd kill him.'

'Bit over the top, Gord.'

Gord gnawed at his lip. 'It isn't, you know. He was in

hospital yesterday.'

'Your dad was? What for?'

'Indigestion.'

Ratso burst out laughing. 'You what?'

Gord coloured. 'Indigestion.'

'What, as in stuffing yourself with food?'

'Got it in one.'

'You mean he actually went to the hospital with a bellyache?'

Gord nodded. 'Don't go on. He thought he'd had a heart attack.'

'Oh, that takes the biscuit,' said Ratso. 'It really does. Wasn't he a bit embarrassed when he found out what was wrong?'

'Red as a beetroot,' Gord answered.

'Going to the hossie with a gut ache,' chortled Ratso. 'Oh, that's a cracker, that is.'

'You let on about this,' Gord warned him, 'and I'll kill you.'

'So it isn't a good time to get back into the team?'

Gord raised his eyes to heaven. 'Dream on. It was the Diamonds that put him in hospital in the first place.'

'Eh? How do you work that out?'

'I was trying to get round him,' Gord explained. 'Asking if I could start again. Then he went bright red and collapsed.'

'Crumbs,' said Ratso. 'He mustn't half hate us.'

'Like a cross to a vampire.' said Gord. 'Hell will freeze over before I play for the Diamonds again.'

'He'll lighten up.'

'Dad? No chance. I'm up the Mersey without a paddle.'

Ratso thought of Sunday's game and the fifteen pounds. 'Same here.'

Four

Gord looked up from his copy of *Shoot* as his dad came through the door. Dad had promised a new de-stressed, unflappable and definitely calm Bobby Jones. As far as Gord was concerned, the jury was still out.

'Any news?' asked Mum.

'Not in front of Gordon,' Dad replied. 'And do you have to lounge about on the couch like that?'

Gord sat up. Typical, he thought, I even lie down wrong.

Mum glanced round. 'Change out of your uniform, love. Your dad and I want to talk.'

Gord climbed the stairs and leant over the bannister rail, on the off-chance of hearing something.

'In your room, Gordon,' shouted Dad.

Gord pulled a face. This was Dad making an effort to be calm! He sat on his bed, tugging off his school tie. He'd have liked to wrap it round his dad's neck. This new leaf he'd turned over since his scare, it looked just like the old leaf. Gord looked up at his poster of Duncan Ferguson. 'Bet you never get kicked around,' he murmured.

With that, he stood up and changed into his tracksuit. He was about to leave his uniform strewn on the floor as usual when he remembered Ratso's money. He bent down and put his hand in the back pocket. It was empty.

'It can't be!'

He checked the other pockets. Then his shirt pocket. Nothing.

'But I can't have dropped it. Think, Gord. Where could it have fallen out?'

Then his heart sank. Oh no, not the couch. A hot flush spread over his neck and shoulders. He could hear

Mum and Dad talking in the living room. If the three fivers were on the couch they were bound to see them.

Gord ran his hand over his face. His fingers were trembling.

'There's only one thing for it,' he told himself. 'I've got to go down there.'

He crept down the stairs and hovered uncertainly outside the living room.

'Is that you, Gordon?'

'Yes, I … I forgot my *Shoot*.'

'You can come in anyway,' said Dad. 'We've something to tell you.'

'Is it bad news?'

'Depends how you look at it,' said Dad.

Gord saw two of the fivers on the couch where he'd been lying and the third poking out of the cushions. Dad was right. He ought to sit up straight. Gord plonked himself down hurriedly. Right on top of the money.

'How do you mean?'

'Well, the Liverpool office is staying open,' Dad explained. 'But I'll have to take a drop in pay. This chap from Manchester got my job.'

Gord slid a hand under his thigh and felt for the money. Then Mum looked straight at him. He slid his hand out and rested it nervously on his knee.

'So something's got to give,' she said. 'It's either the conservatory or the holiday.'

'And your mum and I think it's better to put money into bricks and mortar,' said Dad. 'It'll increase the value of the house.'

Gord made another bid for the cash, but again he was interrupted.

'So we can't go to America?' Gord asked.

'I'm afraid not, son,' said Mum.

Gord could feel the notes under him. It was as if they were burning through the seat of his pants.

'I know you'll be disappointed,' Mum continued, 'but there's nothing we can do.'

Just then, Gord was more worried about Ratso's money.

'That's all right, Mum. I understand.'

'Well, what a mature young man,' she said. 'I'm so proud of you.'

She sat on the couch next to him and pulled him to her for a hug. As Gordon was made to lean forward he saw his dad's expression change.

'Gordon,' said Dad, pouncing on the fivers. 'What's this?'

'Oh, don't make me do this, Dad.'

Dad was stamping round the living room. He must already be up to Stress Warp Nine. 'Where did you put the car keys?'

'They're on the telephone table,' Mum told him. 'Where *you* left them. Bobby, do you really think this is the best way? Remember what the doctor said.'

'No son of mine handles stolen money,' said Dad. 'Now get your jacket on, Gordon, and we'll go and confront Mr Ratcliffe.'

'Not in front of the lads, Dad. Please.'

'If he's down at South Road training, then that's where we're going.'

'But Dad ...'

'I've heard enough out of you. Stealing is wrong. Full stop. End of story. There are no excuses for taking something that doesn't belong to you.'

'Oh, Bobby,' said Mum. 'Aren't you taking this a bit far? It's a childhood prank. I'm sure young Peter didn't mean to steal. And you really must remember your blood pressure.'

'Prank, you call it? That's the trouble these days. Everybody makes excuses for wrongdoing. Well, I think they ought to throw the book at these young thieves. I really do.'

'Bobby,' said Mum. 'Will you please calm down? You're going to burst a blood vessel. Besides, you'll make a fool of yourself.'

Dad held up the money. '*I'm* not the one who's made a fool of myself. Am I, Gordon?'

Gordon hung his head and followed his dad to the car. He remembered what Ratso had said to him. *I owe you one.*

Not any more he didn't.

Five

We couldn't believe our eyes when Bobby and Gord turned up at South Road. It was more the way they arrived, really. Even Ronnie was gob-smacked and it takes a lot to throw him. Bobby appeared frogmarching poor Gord towards us. We all wondered what was going on – except Ratso. He already knew. His face just drained of blood.

It was only later that I was able to piece the whole story together from what Gord and Ratso told me, so this is what you need to know. Bobby takes for South Road, stopping on the way for petrol. He calls in at the nearest petrol station. And who's on duty? Only Ratso's mum. Now, she's in a real old paddy. She's asked Franny if he's the one who's been borrowing money out of her purse and he goes wild, bawling and yelling and saying how dare she accuse him. Anyway, Ratso's mum, she might have let him walk all over her so far, but she isn't the sort of lady to let anybody treat her like a doormat for long. The boys have been on the receiving end of Franny's bullying, but this is her first time. And she doesn't like it.

The next you know, there's a full scale row and she says to Franny: 'I've just split up with one feller who messed me about. You're as bad as Sean. Get your things and go.' And that's that. She's come to work at the petrol station, still fuming after her row with Mein Pigface. So that's the sort of mood she's in when Bobby fills up, jumps into the car and drives off. Just like that. He's so wound up, he forgets to pay. As for Gord, he tries to tell his dad, but Bobby just isn't listening. Too intent on his anti-Ratcliffe mission. He tells Gord he's done enough for one day.

'No son of mine gets involved in stealing,' he yells.

Meantime Ratso's mum is serving another customer when she sees this car pulling away without paying.

'Look at that,' she says. 'That's the third driver this month. I'm phoning the police.' Which is exactly what she does. Everything's set for fun and games down at South Road.

Six

Ratso watched in despair as Bobby came marching across the training pitch.

'I want a word with you, Peter.'

Ronnie looked questioningly at Ratso.

'I'd like you to explain these.'

Gord's dad was holding up three five-pound notes. 'Well?'

'They fell out of my pocket, Ratso,' said Gord miserably. 'I'm sorry.'

'You keep quiet, Gordon,' snapped his dad. 'It's this young rogue I'm talking to.'

Ronnie had been quiet until then, but his patience was wearing thin. 'What's going on here, Bobby?'

'Ask him,' said Gord's dad.

Ronnie glanced at Ratso.

'It's my money,' said Ratso. 'I asked Gord to hang on to it for a couple of days for me.'

'Ah,' said Gord's dad. 'But why?'

Ratso stared at Gord. Gord just hung his head.

'Well?'

It was Ratso's turn to hang his head.

'Well, whose is it?' asked Ronnie.

'Tell him,' said Gord's dad, towering over Ratso. 'Go on. The truth, mind. None of your lies.'

'Let the lad tell me, Bobby,' said Ronnie. He didn't like Bobby Jones at the best of times, but particularly not when he was bullying one of the team.

'I took it out of my mum's purse,' Ratso admitted. 'I couldn't think of any other way to settle the bet.'

'Bet, what bet?'

Ratso was getting ready for a long explanation, but he was cut off by the sound of a police siren on South Road.

'Hear that?' said Gord's dad. 'It's all the time on this estate. A thieves' den, that's what it is round here.' He gave Gord a knowing stare, just to reinforce the point.

'Now that's not fair,' said Ronnie. 'Most of the people round here are honest and hard-working. You can't lump everyone together like that.'

'Oh can't I?' said Gord's dad.

The wail of the siren came closer. Everyone turned as a police car slowed down outside the community centre.

'Eh,' said Guv. 'I think it's coming in here.'

The police officer in the passenger seat was inspecting the number plate on Bobby Jones' car.

'What the devil's he doing?' Gord's dad said out loud.

Then the police car pulled in next to Gord's dad's car. The officer who'd been checking the registration got out and walked steadily towards the pitch. He read the number out slowly.

'Does anyone here own this car?' he asked.

'Why yes,' said Gord's dad. 'I do. Why?'

'I'd like you to accompany me to the police car, sir,' said the policeman. 'I've got some questions for you.'

Gord saw his dad's face turning red, then vivid scarlet. For a moment he thought he was going to have another of his attacks. 'There must be some mistake.'

But there wasn't. Gord followed at a safe distance, with Ratso not far behind. The policeman stopped and turned to face Gord's dad. 'Did you fill up at the Drivewell this evening, sir?'

The red face was turning almost purple. Desperate, haunted eyes were flicking wretchedly in the direction of the Diamonds. 'Yes, I did as a matter of fact. What's all this about?'

'Do you have a receipt for the purchase of the petrol?'

The penny dropped at last. 'Oh my God!'

There was another shamed glance at Ronnie and the boys.

'We got a call from the attendant on duty, sir, a Mrs Ratcliffe.'

Ratso stared.

'It appears you drove off without paying.'

Guv started laughing, but a glare from Ronnie put a stop to that.

'But it was an honest mistake,' stammered Gord's

dad. 'I didn't mean to drive away like that. In fact I was trying to sort out a theft, not commit one.'

There was no change in the policeman's expression.

Gord watched his dad floundering. 'I don't do that sort of thing. I've had a lot on at work, then this trouble with the boys.'

But the policeman wasn't interested in the boys, just a Mr Robert Jones who had driven off without paying.

Gord smiled grimly.

'What's up with you?' asked Ratso. 'What are you grinning at?'

Gord was wondering what Dad would say when he told him the petrol station attendant was the same woman he'd had a row with a couple of weeks before. He was also remembering what his dad had said: *There are no excuses for taking something that doesn't belong to you.*

Suddenly there were no end of excuses.

Seven

Into the valley of death ...

Ratso stood in front of the house. He checked the time. She was bound to be back from work. So how to tell her? It was like the first time he'd swum without armbands. One part of him said he had to face Mum, but nine parts said: *You can't, you can't, you can't.*

He shoved open the gate, wincing at the scrape of the wood on the cracked paving stones. He'd be there, slimy, disgusting Franny urging her on, winding her up against him.

'Peter.' She was putting out the bin bags for collection the next morning. She was still in the red and white overall she wore for work. 'What are you hanging round out there for?'

'It was me, Mum.'

She frowned. 'What?'

He produced the three fivers.

'I think you'd better come inside, Peter.'

Ratso looked around the living room. 'Where's Franny?'

Mum ran her hands through her dyed blonde hair. 'Gone.'

'Gone. Gone where?'

'Gone. Slung his hook. I asked if he'd touched the money. He flipped his lid. I told him to get his things. Simple, really.'

'Oh Mum, I'm sorry.'

She sat on the couch clutching the money he'd handed her. 'I should hope so. What was the money for?'

He explained about the bet. She ranted for a few minutes, threatened him with permanent grounding, that sort of thing, but her heart didn't seem in it.

'You silly, silly lad,' she said finally.

Ratso was aware of Dale and Aaron hovering at the door, eavesdropping. He might have expected that. Nosy beggars. What he hadn't expected was the way Mum took it. She hardly told him off at all. Very strange.

'Aren't you angry with me?'

'I'm angry with myself.'

Ratso stared at her. He didn't understand.

'Something like this was bound to happen. Let's face it, I've been neglecting you.'

Ratso smiled encouragingly. 'Don't be soft, Mum. I was the one who took the money.'

'Why did you do it, though? That's the important thing.'

'I needed it,' said Ratso simply. 'Any ...'

'Yes?'

'I think I wanted to get back at you. You know ...'

Mum nodded wearily.

'Can I ask you something, Mum?'

Curiosity had got the better of his brothers. Dale and Aaron were edging into the room, and Jason had arrived from the kitchen with a sandwich.

'Of course you can, love.'

'Is it my fault, Franny leaving like that?'

Mum shook her head. 'It didn't help, but I think the whole thing was a mistake anyway. It's better to find out now, rather than in a few months time when he's made himself a fixture. I suppose I was feeling low after your dad walked out. I've been a silly old fool.'

'You're not old.'

She smiled. 'That's not what you've been telling your dad. Mutton dressed up as lamb, that's what he says.'

Ratso winced. You couldn't trust Dad with anything. And what a horrible thing to call her. She was still the best mum in the world. Despite everything.

Jason added his opinion. 'That's only because he didn't like seeing you with Franny.'

'Still,' said Mum. 'I can't go round acting like a silly schoolgirl. Did I look *that* stupid?'

Suddenly, Ratso didn't know how to feel. He'd been dying for Franny to clear off, but the way Mum was talking made him uncomfortable. He felt really mean. Like he'd spoilt things for her. Judging by their faces, his brothers felt the same.

'We don't mind you going out,' said Jason. 'Just not with Mein Pigface.'

'Who?'

Jason looked embarrassed. 'Franny.'

'Oh, is that what you called him? So who do you want me to go out with? Maybe you could draw up an approved list. Start with Warren Beatty and work down to Joe Royle.'

Jason shifted his feet uneasily.

Only Dale had an answer. 'What about Dad?'

Suddenly Mum's face was hard. 'What about him?'

Ratso gave Dale a dirty look, but that didn't stop him. 'He could always come back.'

Ratso tried to kick him and make him shut up, but he got Aaron instead.

'Ow!'

'Now what?' asked Mum.

Aaron shot a hurt look at Ratso. 'Nothing.'

'Anyway,' said Mum. 'Enough about my private life. I've got the money back and you're shot of Franny. Maybe we can get on with our lives without any more bother.'

But she hadn't told the telephone that. It trilled shrilly from the hall. 'Now what?'

Ratso was about to turn the TV on when he heard her voice.

'That's right. It happened at the end of my shift. He drove straight off, bold as brass.'

For a few moments she was listening to the voice at the other end, and Ratso was looking for somewhere to hide.

Then: 'At least they got him.'

She replaced the receiver and sat down with a magazine.

'Mum,' said Ratso, his backbone starting to liquify. 'There's something I ought to tell you.'

What followed was a long and involved plea for mercy on behalf of Bobby Jones. Not that Ratso gave a toss for the stuck-up blurt, but he knew Gord could do without any more aggro.

'So you know this feller?' asked Mum as he finished his tale.

Ratso nodded. 'That's right. He used to run the footy team. You know, the one we were always grumbling about. It's Gord's dad. You know him, too.'

'I do?'

'According to Gord, you do. He says you had a few words with him recently. You asked him to hurry up because customers were waiting and he told you to mind your own business.'

Mum rolled her eyes. 'So that's him, is it? Anyway, I'm giving the police a statement tomorrow morning. Are you really asking me to go easy on this Bobby Jones character?'

Ratso nodded.

'He's not a very nice man.'

'He's a moron.'

'And he stole.'

Ratso bit his lip. 'So did I.'

There was a long pause, while Mum let this sink in.

'OK, son,' she said finally. 'Convince me. I'm all ears.'

Eight

I suppose you think I was just kicking my heels all this time. Well, think again. I'm the Guv'nor, and if I don't exactly make dreams come true, at least I make things happen. OK, OK, so I fouled up over Gord and Ratso. But no way was I going to do it again. This time I was focused.

It was just a matter of a little heart-to-heart with Ronnie.
Nothing like a well-timed word in the old shell-like for
kicking things into gear. I did all the talking. All Ronnie
could say was: 'Really?' and 'I see' and 'That explains a
few things' and, finally, 'Fair enough, I'll give her a ring'.

And what did I say? I'm not telling. Well, in football
you've got to have a bit of suspense, haven't you?

Nine

'Got the money, then?' asked Nosmo the moment
Ratso walked into the changing rooms.

'No.'

'Come again.'

Ratso smiled inside at the shocked look on Nosmo's
face. He must have thought he had more face than Big
Ben.

'I didn't bother. We're going to beat you.'

'And if you don't? We had a deal, remember.'

'If we don't, you can have the money and I'll lick the
pavement clean all the way from Goodison to Anfield.'

Nosmo gave Ratso a wary look. The kid was a couple
of sausages short of a fried breakfast.

Guv and Nosmo crossed in the corridor. 'So what did
he want?' Guv asked Ratso.

'He was making sure the bet was still on.'

'And is it?'

'I haven't got the money.'

He remembered the fruitless visit to Dad's flat. No,
he wouldn't give him the money. He should have more
sense.

Guv smiled. 'Then we'll just have to win, won't we?'

Ratso stared gloomily at the floor. All the bravado

he'd mustered for Nosmo's benefit had faded away. 'Forgotten last Sunday, have you?'

'No,' said Guv. 'I just learnt a few lessons from it.'

'Such as?'

'You don't leave big gaps in a flat back four.'

'So how are you going to close them up?' asked Ratso. 'Polyfilla?'

Guv tapped the side of his nose with his finger. 'You'll see.'

Ratso changed into his kit. The usual banter was going on all round him, but he wasn't part of it. It was good that Franny had gone, but his departure didn't seem to have solved anything. Ratso had mentioned it to Dad, but he didn't seem to care. 'It's her life,' he'd said. But it isn't, thought Ratso. It's ours. Then there was still the little matter of the money for the bet. Or rather, the lack of it. He began to wish he hadn't wound up Nosmo so much.

'Come on, lads,' said Ronnie. 'If we can take three points, and Red House come off the field with anything less than a win, we're off the bottom.'

Ratso looked up. That was his line, but he wasn't in the mood.

'Come on, Rats,' said Guv. 'So where's the music?

Ratso clicked in the tape. *Another one bites the dust.* Only it looked like it would be the Diamonds. He watched as Mattie jogged on to the field.

Then it happened. 'Oi, Mattie,' said Ronnie, 'where do you think you're going?'

Mattie frowned. 'What are you on about?'

'Didn't Ronnie mention it?' said Guv. 'There's a team change.'

From behind the changing rooms Gord appeared. His mum was with him.

'Gord Almighty!' said Ratso. 'But how?'

'Just the little matter of a captain's recommendation,' said Guv.

'And a manager's phone call,' added Ronnie.

'Phone call,' Ratso repeated. 'What phone call?'

'To ours,' said Gord. 'Ronnie called us last night.'

'You mean your dad's actually going to let you play!'

'It wasn't Bobby that Ronnie phoned,' said Gord's mum. 'It was me.'

'Mum was brilliant,' said Gord. 'The way she talked to my dad. If you don't let the boy play, she said, you'll be back in hossie. But not with indigestion.'

'You said that, Mrs Jones?' gasped Ratso. 'To Bobby?'

'I did,' said Gord's mum, finding the attention flattering. 'And I should have done it years ago.'

'So how did he take it?' asked Ratso.

'He took it,' said Gord's mum simply. 'I didn't leave him much option. He's a bit less cocky since that petrol station business. It's about time I stood up to him. You know something? It felt good.'

'What did the coppers say to him?' asked Guv.

'Let him off with a good talking to,' said Gord. 'Thanks to Ratso's mum. She went easy on him. Said he'd looked a bit harassed.'

'I bet he was pig sick,' said Ratso. He was gloating, just a bit.

'Not half,' said Gord, as disloyally as he could.

'I think it's time to get off this subject,' said his mum. She was clearly starting to feel uncomfortable. Bobby was still her husband.

'Fair enough,' said Guv. 'Come on, lads. We've got a match to play.'

'Now listen,' said Ronnie. 'This is a tough one, but it isn't beyond you. You've got the skill, but you've got two big disadvantages. You know the first ...'

'Too right,' said Guv. 'We give too much away at the back.' He was staring at Mattie, but Matt was taking little notice. He was crestfallen over being relegated to sub.

'I think Gord can make a difference there,' said Ronnie. 'Just so long as you use the strength you've got. I'm more worried about the age difference. Longmoor are all High School lads, right at the top of the age limit. 'You lot ...' he tousled Joey Bannen's mop of dark hair, 'you're the runts of the litter. Barely eleven yet. So it's no use trying to mix it with them. You'll come a cropper if you do.'

Ronnie had his eye on Guv.

'What are you looking at me for?' Guv demanded. 'I can keep a lid on it.'

Ratso chuckled. 'As the volcano said to the Roman town.'

'Anyway,' said Ronnie. 'I know they've been needling you about this bet.'

The smile vanished from Ratso's face.

'Put that to the back of your minds. It's pace you need today, and accuracy. Find your man with your passes and don't give it away unnecessarily. That's about it.'

The Diamonds were chasing the match from the start. They had a scare right from the kick-off. Nosmo had seen Daz off his line and launched it from forty yards. Daz only just managed to get back and palm it on to the top of the crossbar and out for a corner.

'That's the difference between us,' Nosmo boasted to his mates for Ratso's benefit. 'You need skill for a lob like that.'

Ratso was not amused.

Nor was Guv. 'See that?' he snarled. 'That's what

happens when we get caught napping. Now get your minds on the job.'

Ronnie nodded approvingly.

For the next ten minutes it was all about survival. Ronnie had it right about the age difference, up to two years in the case of Bashir, the Diamonds' youngest player.

Longmoor had done their homework and they had two men on him right from the kick-off. He got sandwiched more often than an egg mayonnaise filling. Guv tried to defend him and pushed one of the markers in the back. It earned him a stern lecture from the referee.

Ronnie was less approving about that part of his game. 'Remember my instructions. Pass and move. No rough stuff. You'll only come off worse in the long run.'

Ant and Dave were on his wavelength at least, passing the ball smoothly out of midfield. There was just one problem. The Diamonds had only got Jamie up front. Dave and Guv were both needed to cover the defence.

'Hold the line, lads,' said Guv. 'They'll tire.'

Nosmo overheard him. 'You wish, McGovern. We're having that fifteen quid, you know.'

Ratso scowled. He didn't like being reminded how easily they'd got a rise out of him.

Longmoor had the ball again. The Diamonds seemed incapable of putting more than three passes together. Longmoor were always harrying them. Pressure, that was the name of their game. Nosmo was the link man for them. He held up the ball then lofted it.

Guv saw the danger. 'Gord, get into him.'

The Longmoor wing-back was already past Jimmy Mintoe and coming infield. Gord tried to tackle but was barged off roughly.

'You all right, Gord?' asked Ratso.

'It's my ribs.' Gord struggled to his feet, wincing. 'He's strong as a flipping ox.'

But Gord's ribs hurt less than his pride. The attack had exposed their lack of muscle and had nearly let Longmoor in for the first goal. Only the woodwork had saved the Diamonds.

Ratso was the next player to take on his opposite number and come off worst. Ripped apart by the speed of the Longmoor break, they were wide open. Nosmo had the ball on the edge of the area.

Ratso slid in a tackle, but Nosmo saw it coming. He just dropped his shoulder, moved inside and hit a rising shot.

One-nil to Longmoor.

'You'll have to get up early in the morning to take me with a tackle like that,' said Nosmo. 'You'd better start counting that cash, lad.'

Ratso was furious. At himself, mostly.

Luckily for the Diamonds, Daz was playing a blinder. He couldn't have done much about the goal, but he dealt with everything else that came his way. One save in particular was out of this world. One of the Longmoor forwards hit a screamer low, and at the foot of the post. Daz dived and pushed it aside with his finger tips. It was a pure reaction save.

'We're getting hammered,' panted Gord.

'I know,' said Ratso. 'We're lucky to be only one-nil down.'

Guv wasn't impressed by the match analysis. 'They're going to tire,' he insisted stubbornly. 'You watch.'

But Longmoor came again, outpacing Joey and Ant and setting up Nosmo for another shot. Daz got to it but took the full force of Nosmo's shot in the face. He crumpled to the deck.

'Are you all right, Daz?' asked Joey.

Daz didn't answer. He just sat up and grinned ruefully. 'I'm going to have a nose like Peter Schmeichel.'

'Tiring, are they?' Ratso asked Guv. 'Well, I'm still watching.'

Guv gave as good as he got. 'Well stop watching and start playing.'

'Cheeky devil!' said Ratso.

'He's right, though,' said Gord. 'We've got to lift our game.'

'Oh yeah? How?'

Guv looked at Ronnie. The manager was pointing at Bash and gesturing towards the right of the pitch. Guv nodded.

'What's all that about?' asked Gord.

Ratso tapped his forehead. 'Ronnie wants him to change wings. Good move.'

It was. Bashir suddenly had some space. He took the ball to the line and dropped a cross into the area. Jamie flew in and drilled in a header. He was unlucky to find the angle of the bar and upright and see his effort bounce out.

Ronnie gave the thumbs up. 'More like it.'

But Longmoor weren't caught wrong-footed for long. They picked up Bash in his new position and neutralized the threat. Ratso saw Carl and Mattie following the match keenly. They were watching Gord's every move, hoping for a slip.

Just before half-time Nosmo picked up the ball out on the left and looked up. Gord sized up the situation. Everybody was marked. He was certain there was nothing on.

—— 125 ——

'Gord, you divvy. Pick up the runner.'

Alerted by Guv's shout, Gord turned and saw one of the Longmoor defenders coming from deep. Gord knew what he had in mind. He was going to chest it down and run on into the area. Gord threw himself at the runner and lashed at the ball. Unfortunately, he caught the player in the chest and watched as he crashed to the ground.

'See that, ref,' yelled Nosmo. 'What an animal!'

'I didn't mean it,' said Gord. 'I was going for the ball.'

'I've got my eye on you, son,' warned the ref. 'Another tackle like that and you're in the book.'

The Longmoor player hobbled to his feet and sized Gord up. 'Come near me again and you'll get more than a booking, lad.'

Nosmo was standing with his foot on the ball. He chipped it suddenly and found a colleague. The attacking player was spring-heeled. He rose above Ant and headed home.

Two-nil at half-time.

Ten

I was having doubts, I don't mind telling you. Two down at half-time and against one of the tightest defences in the league. We'd hardly been in the game. I still believed we were on the right lines, though. Sure, Longmoor were giving us the run-around, but we'd held them to two goals. There weren't many teams that could claim that. By half-time Longmoor had usually run away with it and were getting ready to put on an exhibition in the second half. At least with us, they still knew they had a game on their hands.

Mattie was trying to make out that Gord had been to

blame for the second goal. Tell it to the marines, I said. He had to go for the ball. He was unlucky, that's all. The only thing that worried me was whether he would lose his bottle. Longmoor had been giving him earache over the high challenge. We were going to see what he was made of in the second half.

We did get one boost, though, or at least Ratso did. His mum and dad turned up during the interval. Well, everybody likes a bit of moral support, even me. I wasn't half glad of Mum and Gareth on the touch-line. Ratso's mum and dad were together, and all. From what Ratso had told me, you couldn't get them on the same planet, never mind the same footy pitch. Suddenly, there they were. Ratso's mind must have been doing overtime. The Ratsos had his brothers in tow, all except the big one.

It was the look on the brothers' faces that cracked me up. Like they believed their parents were really going to get back together.

I tell you, I've lived some and I don't believe in fairy stories.

Eleven

The Diamonds continued to hang on. Just. A lot of that was down to Ratso. His parents' arrival had given him a lift and he was tackling like a terrier. Longmoor laughed at him at first.

'Look at this scrawny little runt,' they said.

But Ratso soon wiped the smile off their faces. Nosmo got the ball in front of goal. He took it in his stride and he was about to blast it when Ratso came in from the side. Nosmo threw himself to the floor and started rolling about Italian-fashion, but it was a fair challenge. The ref waved play on.

'Ref,' Nosmo appealed as he rose to his knees. 'Tackle from behind.'

'Behave,' said Guv. 'You ought to get an Oscar for that dive.'

At the other end Bashir was operating in midfield. He'd dropped back to find some space. For once his markers hadn't come with him.

'Bash,' shouted Dave. 'On the floor.'

Bashir nodded and whipped it in low. The cross was inch-perfect and Dave volleyed it home with relish.

Two-one down and twenty minutes to go.

'Still think you've got it in the bag?' asked Ratso cheekily.

'Lucky effort,' snorted Nosmo.

Ratso glanced in his parents' direction. They were still talking. Smiling even. And he could have sworn their arms touched. This was unreal.

'Bit of a turn-up for the book, isn't it?' asked Gord.

'Tell me about it,' said Ratso. 'The last I knew, Dad was exiled to the primeval slime.'

'Come again?'

Ratso chuckled. 'Don't you have dictionaries in your house?'

'You two going to gas-bag all day?' demanded Guv.

'Sorry,' said Gord.

'Don't apologize,' said Guv severely. 'Play.'

Gord tracked his marker across the centre of the pitch. His opponent was a tall skinhead who used his elbows in every challenge. Gord remembered Ronnie's advice: Don't mix it. That was OK in other areas of the field, but not in defence. He had to show this skinhead who was boss. Whether it went down well or not. If he didn't quell the threat quickly, the Diamonds were going to get punished again. He saw Nosmo working the ball out of defence. Skinhead made his run as Nosmo launched a long ball in his direction. Gord watched for the elbows and got ahead of his man, heading it out of play for a corner.

'Nice interception, Gord,' said Guv.

The corner came over, a high inswinger. Daz started to come then stopped. It was dropping over his head.

'Mine!' yelled Skinhead.

'Mine!' bawled Gord, determined to close his man down.

The next thing Gord knew there was a sickening crack and he was lying in the goal itself, tangled up in the net.

'You all right?' Ratso was asking through a grey mist.

'Ye-es,' Gord replied uncertainly. 'Did I clear it?'

'Oh yeah,' said Guv. 'You cleared it. Him too.'

His opponent was lying face down in the box.

'What's up?' asked Gord. 'Why isn't he moving?'

'Clash of heads,' said Ronnie, bending over. 'Look at me, Gord. Any dizziness?'

'No, I'm fine. What about him?'

Ronnie looked over at the Longmoor coach.

'He's dazed,' said their manager. 'I'd better run him to casualty. Just in case.'

'Maybe I ought to take our Gordon, too,' said his mum.

'Don't you dare, Mum,' said Gord. 'I've got a game to win.'

She glanced anxiously at Ronnie. 'Your decision, Mrs Jones, but I think he's OK.'

Gord's mum thought for a moment. 'All right, but any dizziness or blurred vision and you tell me, Gordon.'

'Yeah yeah.'

As the match restarted, Nosmo found Gord. 'That's the second of our lads you've flattened. Watch yourself.'

'But it was an accident.'

'You're the one who'll have an accident.'

Gord watched Nosmo stalking away.

'Forget it,' said Ant. 'It's all talk.'

But it wasn't. Gord had two players on him all the time. Whenever he went for the ball they brought him crashing to the ground. Half the tackles were off the ball.

'Come on, ref,' called Guv. 'Give him some protection.'

The ref had a word with the two boys, but it didn't have much effect. A couple of minutes later, Gord was trying to steer the ball out to Bashir when they crashed into him from behind.

Guv was in like a flash. 'Leave him alone,' he yelled. 'Or I'll sort you out.'

'You and whose army?'

Seeing Guv outnumbered, Ratso joined the confrontation.

'That's out of order,' he yelled. 'That was a fifty-fifty ball when Gord went in with your lad. You've no complaint.'

'That's enough,' said the ref. 'Calm down or I'll be getting the book out.'

Guv gave the ref a sceptical glance. There were only so many times you could threaten to use the book. This feller was useless.

Within a minute Gord was in trouble again. He was challenging for the ball when Nosmo elbowed him in the face. When Gord got up his nose was pouring with blood.

'Gordon,' cried his mum, but he was already waving

her back to her place on the touch-line.

'Stand still,' said Ronnie. He started squeezing the bridge of Gord's nose.

'Did you see that?' Guv was shouting at the referee. 'He smacked Gord in the face for nothing.'

'I saw it all right,' said the ref. 'Now you go over there and I'll deal with it.'

Guv backed off reluctantly.

Gord saw the anguished look on Nosmo's face. He'd got his marching orders.

'Want to change the bet?' asked Ratso mischievously as Nosmo took the long walk. 'How's about twenty quid?'

'Get stuffed.'

'Right,' said Ronnie. 'The bleeding's stopped.' He turned towards the touch-line. Mattie was peeling off his trackie top.

'What are you doing?' asked Gord.

'Bringing Mattie on. You've had two bad knocks.'

'He comes on over my dead body,' said Gord.

Ronnie looked surprised. So soft lad *could* take it. 'Your choice, son. You definitely want to play on?'

'Of course he wants to play on,' said Guv. 'Steel in your soul, haven't you, Gord? He can take it, Ronnie.'

'I'm talking to Gord,' said Ronnie. 'Now you're sure you want to play on?'

Gord nodded.

'We've got a man over,' said Guv excitedly. 'Let's make it count.'

A turning point had been reached. Longmoor had lost their organizer and were looking ragged. The Diamonds however looked fresh and sharp.

Ratso found himself in the centre circle with acres of room.

'Take it on,' shouted Guv. 'We've a man over.'

Ratso did as he was told. He was cautious at first, but as the space opened up in front of him he saw the opportunity. Pushing the ball forward, he ran right to the edge of the area.

'Hit it!' screamed Gord.

But Dave was making a run to Ratso's left and he was completely unmarked. Shifting his weight, Ratso rolled it into Dave's path. All Dave had to do was side-foot home.

Two-all.

'Brilliant!' yelled Ronnie. 'Completely selfless.'

Ratso pulled his shirt over his head, Ravanelli-style, and ran twenty yards in celebration before yanking it off his face. He saw his mum and dad cheering.

'Excellent, Peter,' said Ronnie. 'Simply excellent.'

'Thanks,' said Ratso. 'A player's player, that's me.'

Gord leapt on his back, ragging him. 'Don't overdo it,' he said. 'We all know you're brilliant.'

But the game wasn't over yet. Longmoor had one more ace up their sleeve. They brought on a tall boy with longish blond hair.

'Watch him,' warned Guv. 'He's fast. He plays for our school.'

'So how come he's only sub?'

'No stamina,' said Guv. 'But in short bursts, he's awesome.'

'Then put Bash on him,' said Gord. 'Speed for speed. I'll cover.'

'That's not a half bad idea,' said Guv. 'We'll do it.'

Blondie got the ball a few seconds later. Gord had been right to ask for backup. The boy left him for dead. Not Bash, though. He hared after him and managed to get in a half-challenge on the edge of the box. It gave Gord just enough time to recover. He came in hard and brought the ball away. It was the third

Longmoor player he'd flattened, but this time there were no complaints.

Longmoor had shot their bolt.

'Gord,' shouted Dave. 'My ball.'

Gord had seen Ronnie signal full time. It hardly seemed worth even trying to mount an attack, but he passed the ball anyway. You never knew with Dave. Like Guv always said, his feet had been kissed by the angels. Dave was on the halfway line and his way was barred by two defenders. The two Diamonds front players were well-marked. He had nowhere to go. Then Dave glanced up and saw the Longmoor goalie off his line. With a toss of the head he hit the ball.

'Now that's a waste of a ball,' grumbled John O'Hara, positive as usual.

'I'm not so sure,' said Ratso.

'Good grief,' cried Gord. 'It's on target.'

The ball was dropping fast and the Longmoor goalie was back-pedalling desperately. It was a carbon copy of Nosmo's first-half effort, but this time the goalie was floundering.

'It's going in,' yelled Guv.

He was right. To everyone's astonishment, it ended up nestling in the back of Longmoor's net.

The Diamonds had won a famous three-two victory.

Twelve

It was a stunner, the sort of goal that you score once in a lifetime. Pele tried it in 1970 and David Beckham actually did it for Man U in 1996. But Dave Lafferty's one of ours. It was the perfect ending to the most hard-fought match we'd ever played.

What's more, my gambles had paid off. Gord was like a rock at the heart of our defence. Even better, he was a rock who gave as good as he got. He came off with a black eye and a bloody nose but I don't think I've ever seen him so happy.

Ratso came to life as well. No jokes, no fooling around, he ran his heart out. He's no Dave Lafferty and he'll never be more than a functional player, but you couldn't have asked for more. The scrawny little rat was a tiger. Oh, and one more thing about Ratso. Remember what I said about his mum and dad? Well, it looks like I was wrong. Sometimes you do get a fairy tale ending. Even on the Diamond.

I'll be working for a fairy tale ending to the season too, you can be sure of that. The lads used to be worms, but I knew they had it in them to change. Well, that's what they've done. They're diamonds. Diamonds.

Thirteen

'You know something?' Ratso said loudly as he passed a dejected Longmoor side.

'What's that?' asked Nosmo.

'It's about Dave's goal. You need skill to do a lob like that.'

'Very funny,' said Nosmo. He didn't like being made to chew on his own words.

'So have you got our money?' Ratso asked cheerfully.

Nosmo scowled. 'Come to the changing room in five minutes. We'll have to have a whip round.'

'Don't tell me you were expecting to beat us,' said Ratso, teasing the opposition.

'We would have done,' snapped Nosmo. 'Only you didn't play fair.'

'How do you work that out?' demanded Guv. 'You were the only ones kicking players off park.'

'Oh yeah,' said Nosmo. 'So how did Dean end up in that state?'

Gord saw the lad he'd collided with sitting in the manager's car. He looked pale.

'How is he? What did the hossie say?'

'What do you care?' asked Skinhead.

Gord bristled. 'I care, OK?'

'Mild concussion. He'll be fine.'

Longmoor trooped off to get changed.

'Hey, heard the news?' called Jamie.

'What?'

'Red House got tanked eleven-one. We're off the bottom.'

That set everybody off. To the tune of *We're in the Money*, the singing began.

We're off the bottom.

We're off the bottom.

Then deafeningly.

WE'RE OFF THE BOTTOM!

It was a terrific feeling.

'I'm going to see my mum and dad,' said Ratso.

'You're coming back, though?' asked Gord.

'Too right,' said Ratso. 'There's still the little matter of Longmoor's fifteen quid.'

He caught his parents by the front gate. 'Do you mind if I go out with the lads?' he asked. 'We're using the money from the bet to go to McDonald's.'

'Of course we don't mind,' said Mum. 'Just don't go running across that roundabout again.'

Ratso smiled. He liked the way she said *we*.

'Does this mean you're ... ?'

'Back together?' asked Mum.

Ratso nodded. 'Uh-huh.'

She gave Dad a querying look.

'Yes,' he said, wrinkling his nose. 'I think so. And you can even show off your tummy if you want.'

Aaron, Dale and Ratso put their hands to their heads. 'No-o-o-o, anything but that.'

'We'll see you back home, son.'

Ratso smiled. More broadly still. He really did like that *we*.

By the time he got to the changing rooms, Nosmo had the money. Ronnie was there too.

'You can take it this time,' he told Ratso. 'But if anybody's caught gambling again, they're suspended. Got that?'

'Don't worry,' said Ratso. 'It was a one-off.'

'I still say you don't deserve it,' Nosmo grumbled, tossing the fifteen pound coins on the ground.

'Aw,' said Ratso. 'We're really cut up about that.'

'Right,' said Guv. 'McDonald's it is. Everybody ready?'

'Does that include us?' asked a shamefaced Mattie. He was standing with Carl on the edge of the group.

'That depends,' said Guv coolly.

'On what?'

'On whether you're going to leave Gord alone.'

Mattie nodded. 'I suppose so.'

Guv raised an eyebrow.

'Yes,' said Mattie. 'We'll be nice to Gord.'

At the mention of Gord's name Ratso looked around. He was standing with his mum.

'What's up, Gord? Aren't you coming?

Gord looked up at his mum. More in hope than anticipation, he asked her permission. 'Can I, Mum?'

She hesitated for a moment, then smiled. 'Why not?'

Gord couldn't believe his ears. 'You mean it?'

'Yes. Enjoy yourself.'

Gord gave her a hug.

'And be back home by three this afternoon.'

'I will.'

With that, he raced after his team mates. 'I can come. Did you hear me, I can actually come.'

And as one man the boys shouted: 'Gord Almighty!'

Fourteen

So that was it, I was through the pain barrier and I'd brought Gord and Ratso through with me. OK, so they had a bit to do with it too, but I was still the main man, the Guv'nor and don't let anybody forget it. I was feeling really pleased with myself, all in all. There's this saying: you can't make an omelette without breaking eggs. Well, tell me if I'm wrong but I think that's exactly what I'd done. I'd even kept Mattie and Carl on board. They weren't exactly class players but they'd come in as cover for the other lads. I reckoned we'd laid some foundations. We'd ditched Bobby Jones and got ourselves a proper manager. We'd turned Gord into a bit of a rock at the back and even old Ratso seemed to have an appetite for the battle. We were off the bottom of the league and climbing the table. What's more, we were looking forward to a good run in the Challenge Cup. Things were looking up.

Mind you, you're only as good as your last game, and little did I know what was next in store. Just when we seemed to have turned the corner, we were about to face one of our worst set-backs, and from an unlikely source. It wasn't one of the weak links in the side that was going to give me heartache, but one of its pillars of strength.

But that's another story.